'I'm sorry, Molly. I never meant to upset you like this.'

Sean drew her to him once more, planting a gentle kiss on her cheek. It was meant to be no more than a token—a simple expression of gratitude for her support—and it might have remained that way too if she hadn't chosen that precise moment to turn her head.

Molly froze when she felt his lips glide from her cheek and come to rest at the corner of her mouth. She knew that she should do something to stop what was happening, but it was as though her body was suddenly refusing to obey her. When his lips started to move again, deliberately this time, she could only stand there...motionless.

His mouth found hers and she heard him sigh, felt the warm expulsion of his breath on her lips, and it was that which broke the spell. However, if she'd hoped that it would bring her to her senses she was mistaken. Her lips seemed to possess a will of their own as they clung to his, eagerly inviting him to continue. And he did...

Dear Reader,

Once again I have returned to Dalverston General Hospital and used it as the setting for this book. Although the town of Dalverston is purely a figment of my imagination, the area it is based on is one of my favourite parts of the world—the beautiful English Lake District. I always experience a little thrill of pleasure whenever I set a book there.

Molly is shocked when she discovers that Sean Fitzgerald is to be the new locum registrar, covering the busy Christmas and New Year period in Dalverston General's A&E department. When Sean worked there before they had an affair, and it has taken Molly a long time to get over it. To have Sean reappear in her life is the last thing she needs.

Sean knows that he hurt Molly and regrets it deeply—but he had no choice. He's made a solemn vow never to get involved with any woman and he has to keep it. However, seeing Molly again arouses all kinds of emotions and he struggles to remain detached. Can he break his vow and win Molly back, as he yearns to do? Or will he always regret it? Read on to find out!

If you would like to learn more about the background to my Dalverston series then do visit my blog at jennifertaylorauthor.wordpress.com.

Love,

Jennifer

MIRACLE UNDER THE MISTLETOE

BY
JENNIFER TAYLOR

First published in Great Britain 2015
by Mills & Boon, an imprint of Harlequin (UK) Limited,
Eton House, 18-24 Paradise Road, Richmond, Surrey, TW9 1SR

© 2015 Jennifer Taylor

ISBN: 978-0-263-26064-9

Harlequin (UK) Limited's policy is to use papers that are natural,
renewable and recyclable products and made from wood grown in
sustainable forests. The logging and manufacturing processes conform
to the legal environmental regulations of the country of origin.

Printed and bound in Great Britain
by CPI Antony Rowe, Chippenham, Wiltshire

Jennifer Taylor lives in the north-west of England, in a small village surrounded by some really beautiful countryside. She has written for several different Mills & Boon series in the past, but it wasn't until she read her first Medical Romance that she truly found her niche. When she's not writing, or doing research for her latest book, Jennifer's hobbies include reading, gardening, travel, and chatting to friends both on and offline. She is always delighted to hear from readers, so do visit her website at jennifertaylorauthor.wordpress.com.

Books by Jennifer Taylor

Mills & Boon Medical Romance

The Doctor's Baby Bombshell
The Midwife's Christmas Miracle
Small Town Marriage Miracle
Gina's Little Secret
The Family Who Made Him Whole
The Son that Changed His Life
The Rebel Who Loved Her
The Motherhood Mix-Up
Mr Right All Along
Saving His Little Miracle
One More Night with Her Desert Prince...
Best Friend to Perfect Bride

Visit the Author Profile page
at millsandboon.co.uk for more titles.

CHAPTER ONE

'LEFT A BIT…a bit more. No, that's too far now.'

'For heaven's sake, Suzy, make up your mind. I'm starting to get vertigo from balancing on the top of this ladder!'

Molly Daniels rolled her eyes as she looked down at her friend, Suzy Walters. It was the start of her Friday night shift and from the amount of noise issuing from the waiting room things were already hotting up. With just three weeks to go until Christmas, the A&E unit at Dalverston General Hospital was coming under increasing pressure as people set about enjoying the festivities. She really needed to get down to some work so, tossing back her strawberry blonde curls, which as per usual had come loose from their clip, Molly held up the bunch of mistletoe once more.

'How about here? Maybe it's not the exact centre of the room but I doubt if anyone except you will notice that.'

'I suppose it will have to do,' Suzy conceded grudgingly. She grimaced as Molly pinned the rather wilted bunch of foliage to the ceiling above the coffee table. 'Although, according to custom, you are supposed to be standing *under* the mistletoe before anyone can kiss you and you can't do that with the table being there, can you?'

'Well, that's fine by me.' Molly made sure the drawing pin was securely anchored then climbed down from the ladder. 'I've had it with men calling the shots, so if anyone gets any idea about kissing me without my express permission they can forget it!'

'Oh, come on, Molly. You don't really mean that.'

Suzy followed Molly out of the staffroom, a frown furrowing her brow. They had met at university while they had been studying for their nursing degrees and had remained firm friends ever since. Molly knew that Suzy only wanted her to be happy; however, her friend's idea of happiness—i.e. finding the right man to settle down and have a family with, as Suzy herself had done—was no longer hers.

She had tried that and she had the scars to prove it too! Her dream had always been to find her ideal mate so that she could enjoy the kind of loving and supportive relationship her parents had. She had set out her stall accordingly, opting to date men who had possessed the right credentials. They had to be reliable and trustworthy, caring and kind. The problem was that although they had appeared to tick all the right boxes, they had turned out to be far from perfect. One was too bossy,

another too needy, a third too *boring*—and so it had
gone on.

The one and only time she had veered off course and
dated someone who hadn't fitted her brief had been an
even bigger disaster, though. She had had her heart well
and truly crushed then and from now on she intended
to take a very different approach when it came to relationships. There would be no more wondering if this
or that man was Mr Right. And definitely no more sitting by the phone, waiting for him to call. The days of
her being a lovelorn victim were well and truly over!

'I do.' Molly held up her hand when Suzy opened her
mouth to protest. 'Save your breath, Suzy. I've heard
it all before: one day I'll meet the man of my dreams
and ride off into the sunset with him.' Molly snorted in
disgust, her emerald-green eyes filled with cynicism.
'I may have believed in the fairy tale at one time, but
I don't believe it now. The man doesn't exist who can
make me change my mind about that, either!'

Molly spun round and headed to the nurses' station.
Fond as she was of Suzy, she didn't intend to waste any
more time debating the issue. She did the hand-over,
listening closely while Joyce Summers, her opposite
number on the day shift, updated her as to the status
of the patients currently in the unit. As senior sister,
Molly needed to know what stage they were up to in
their treatment. She nodded when Joyce had finished.

'Not too bad, from the sound of it.'

'It's early days yet,' Joyce replied with all the weary

wisdom gained from twenty-odd years spent working on the unit. She was due to retire after Christmas and was looking forward to it immensely.

'It is,' Molly agreed, laughing. 'So how are your plans coming on? Have you booked that cruise you were telling me about?'

'I have indeed. Three weeks in the Caribbean. I can't wait!' Joyce picked up her cardigan and started to leave then paused. 'Oh, I forgot to tell you that we've got a locum covering over Christmas and the New Year. He's starting tonight... Oh, talk of the devil—here he is! At least we know he's up to the job, unlike some I could mention.'

Molly glanced round to see who had come in through the main doors and felt her heart grind to a halt. It couldn't be him, she told herself sickly. Not now, after she had finally sorted out her life. It must be her imagination playing tricks, trying to test her newfound resolve after what she had told Suzy, but it wasn't going to work. Closing her eyes, Molly counted to ten, convinced that when she opened them again the apparition would have disappeared...

'Hello, Molly. Long time, no see, as the saying goes.'

Molly's eyes flew open as she stared at the man standing in front of her. A wave of panic washed over her as she drank in all the familiar details, from the jet-black hair falling over his forehead to the deep blue eyes that were studying her with undisguised amusement. This man had been her one and only aberration.

Even though she had known from the outset that he was far from being her ideal life partner, she had had an affair with him. He had possessed none of the qualities she had always deemed essential in a relationship. On the contrary, he wasn't reliable or trustworthy, and he definitely wasn't looking for commitment, but she had gone ahead anyway and slept with him. Now, as she saw the smile that curved his lips, Molly realised that any hopes she may have harboured about him being a figment of her imagination had been way off beam. Sean Fitzgerald wasn't some kind of hallucination. He wasn't even a memory dredged up from her past. He was completely and utterly real!

Sean managed to hold his smile but it wasn't easy. Although he had guessed that Molly might not be exactly overjoyed to see him again, he hadn't envisaged *this* reaction. As he took stock of the pallor of her skin, he was overcome by a feeling of shame he had never experienced before. It didn't matter that he had made his intentions perfectly clear from their very first date, or that he had frequently reiterated the fact that he didn't intend to commit himself to *anyone*. He had hurt her. Badly.

Sean's heart sank as that thought hit home. He had thought long and hard when the agency had phoned and offered him this post as locum senior registrar on Dalverston's A&E unit. He had been very aware that working with Molly could turn out to be challenging to say the least. His initial reaction had been to turn it down but in the end he had decided to accept it. He needed to work over the Christmas period, needed to be kept busy so that he wouldn't dwell on the past. He couldn't bear to leave it to chance that another post would come up, so he had set aside his qualms and accepted the offer. Now, however, he couldn't help wondering if it had been selfish to put his own needs first.

'I wasn't sure who would be working tonight,' he said lightly, struggling to behave as normally as possible. That was the key to handling this situation, he assured himself. After all, it wasn't the first time that he had found himself working with a woman he had dated and subsequently dumped and he had learned from experience that the best way to defuse matters was by acting normally. All he could do was hope that it would work this time too, although something warned him that he was being overly optimistic.

'No? You should have asked for a copy of the roster. Then you could have opted to work a different shift and avoided me, as I'm sure we both would have preferred.'

Molly's voice sounded harsh and so unlike the tone he remembered that Sean frowned. However, before he could say anything, she picked up a file from the desk and headed towards the waiting room. He watched her go, feeling a whole host of emotions hit him one after the other—slam, bang, wallop: regret, sadness, an unfamiliar sense of loss...

Sean blanked them all out, knowing how pointless it was to go down that route. He had done what he had

had to do: ended their relationship when he had realised that Molly was getting far too attached to him. He had, in effect, done the honourable thing, he assured himself as he headed to the staffroom to deposit his coat. He had called a halt before things had gone too far—although how far was *too* far? he wondered suddenly as he keyed in the security code and unlocked the door. Should he have stopped after their first kiss? Or before they had slept together? And surely he should have called a halt before it had happened a second and a third time, even if making love with Molly had been the most wonderful experience of his life?

The door closed behind him with a noisy thud but he didn't even notice. Making love with Molly had been mind-blowing and there was no point denying it. He had felt things when they had made love that he had never felt before, not even with Claire, and the thought was so painful that he winced. Was that why he had been so brusque when he had ended his relationship with Molly? Because he had felt guilty? Had it seemed like the ultimate betrayal of the woman he had been going to marry to feel all those things for Molly?

Sean knew it was true and it didn't make him feel any better to admit it. For the past ten years he had remained faithful to his dead fiancée. Oh, admittedly, he had slept with many women during that time but he had never become emotionally involved with any of them, and that was what counted. However, it had been different with Molly. She had touched him on so many levels; their affair hadn't been purely physical, as he had wanted it to be.

It made him see that he would need to be very careful while he was working at Dalverston. It would be only too easy to break the vow he had made after Claire had died.

It was a busy night, as Molly had predicted. By the time she was due for her break, the unit was overflowing with people waiting to be seen. She shook her head when Jason Roberts, the newest addition to their staff, asked her if she was going to the canteen.

'I'll wait till things calm down a bit,' she explained then sighed as the doors opened to admit another group of injured revellers. One of them was bleeding copiously from a gash on his forehead. That he was also extremely drunk as well was evident from the way he was staggering about. Molly beckoned to Jason to follow her as she headed straight over to him. In her experience it was better to get the drunks safely corralled so they couldn't upset the rest of their patients.

'Right, let's get you sat down for starters.' She guided the man to a chair and bent down to examine the cut on his head. Although there was a great deal of blood, it was only a superficial injury and would need just butterfly stitches to close it. 'Get him checked in at Reception, will you?' she told Jason. 'Then you can clean this up and apply a few butterfly stitches to hold it together.'

It was a simple enough task and one the young nurse

was more than capable of performing; however, it appeared the patient had other ideas. Grabbing hold of Molly's arm, he pulled her back when she went to leave.

'I want you to do it, not him.' He looked at Jason and sneered. 'I don't want some young kid messing around with me.'

'Jason is a fully qualified nurse. He is more than capable of dealing with this,' Molly explained levelly. She tried to withdraw her arm from the man's grasp but he wouldn't let her go. His fingers tightened around her wrist, making her wince with pain.

'I said that I want you to do it.' He hauled her down so that their faces were mere inches apart and she had to stop herself gagging at the sour smell of alcohol coming off his breath. 'I pay my taxes, love, and if I say I want *you* to treat me then that's how it's going to be.'

'I'm afraid it doesn't work like that, sir. *We* decide who gets to treat you and *we* also decide who we won't treat, either. I have to say that you're number one on that list at this precise moment.'

Molly looked round when she recognised Sean's voice. Although he hadn't raised his voice, there was no disguising the anger on his face. It obviously had an effect on the drunk because he immediately let her go. Molly stepped back, her legs trembling a little as she hastily put some space between them. Although it wasn't the first time that she'd had to deal with an unpleasant situation, it was upsetting, nevertheless.

'Are you all right?'

Sean's voice was low, filled with something that brought an unexpected lump to her throat. He sounded genuinely concerned but that couldn't be right, not after the way he had ended their affair two years ago. He had been almost brutal as he had told her bluntly that he didn't want to see her any more. Although Molly had asked him why, *pleaded* with him to tell her what had made him reach such a decision, he had refused to explain. He had merely reminded her that he had made it clear right from the beginning that he wasn't looking for commitment, and that had been that. He had left Dalverston shortly afterwards to take up another post in a different part of the country and had never made any attempt to contact her since.

Sean had written her out of his life and it would be foolish to imagine that he cared, even more foolish to wish that he did. Even though Molly knew all that, she couldn't stop herself. Foolish or not, she wanted him to care about her and the thought was like the proverbial red rag. As Jason led the drunk away, she rounded on Sean, pain and anger warring inside her. The last thing she wanted was to feel anything for him ever again!

'I would appreciate it if you didn't interfere in future,' she told him furiously. 'I am more than capable of dealing with a situation like that.'

'I'm sorry,' he said quietly. 'I just thought maybe you needed some backup.'

'Well, you thought wrong,' Molly snapped. She

glared at him. 'I don't need your help, Dr Fitzgerald, and I would prefer it if you didn't butt in.'

'Then all I can do is apologise and assure you that it won't happen again.'

He gave her a thin smile then walked away, leaving Molly fuming. She knew she had overreacted and it was frustrating to think that she had allowed Sean to get to her like that. The only way she would cope in the coming weeks while they had to work together was by remaining calm, indifferent even. Allowing her emotions to come to the fore, whether it was anger or anything else, certainly wouldn't help. No, she needed to remain detached, aloof, distant, and that way she would get through this. However, as she went to collect her next patient, Molly was bitterly aware that it wasn't going to be easy to be any of those things. Working with Sean was going to test her self-control to its absolute limit.

CHAPTER TWO

IT WAS A busy night, although not busy enough for Sean's liking. As one patient succeeded another, he found himself wishing for more—some kind of major incident that would mean he didn't have time to think about anything apart from the lives he was saving. It wasn't that he wanted people to get hurt—far from it. However, anything that would stop him thinking about Molly and the way he had reacted when that drunk had grabbed hold of her would be a relief.

'Lily should be fine, but don't hesitate to bring her back if you're at all concerned about her.' He dragged his thoughts back to the present and smiled at the anxious parents of seventeen-year-old Lily Morris. They had brought their daughter into the unit after she had woken during the night with an angry red rash all over her body. They had been worried that she had contracted meningitis but Sean had been able to allay their fears. It turned out that Lily had reacted adversely to some new shower gel she had bought off a market stall;

she would be absolutely fine as long as she didn't use it again.

'Thank you so much, Doctor.' Mr Morris sighed as he shook Sean's hand. 'If it's not one thing, it's another when you have children. Lily gave us a right old scare when we saw the state of her, I can tell you.'

'I'm sure she did but, as I said, Lily should be fine so long as she sticks to her usual shower gel.'

Sean saw the family out then went to the desk and emailed the local Trading Standards office. The gel Lily had purchased had been purportedly a leading brand but he seriously doubted it was genuine. Hopefully, Trading Standards would be able to investigate and stop anyone else purchasing it and ending up in the same state as Lily.

Once that was done, he checked the whiteboard to make sure that nobody had been waiting longer than they should. Government guidelines stated that patients should be seen, treated and either transferred to a ward or sent home within a set number of hours. There was just one patient nearing that limit, so he made his way to Cubicles to check what was happening. The curtains were drawn and he pushed them aside, feeling his heart sink when he found Molly standing beside the bed.

Although they had spoken a couple of times since that incident involving the drunk, Sean had tried his best to stay out of Molly's way. Not only did he want to avoid another confrontation with her, but he wasn't comfortable with all the emotions she seemed to have stirred up inside him. He wanted to be indifferent to her but he knew deep down that it was beyond him. Maybe he had succeeded in dismissing all the other women he had dated from his mind but he couldn't rid himself of Molly, it seemed.

'How's it going in here, Sister?' he asked, falling back on professional courtesy seeing as everything else seemed way too difficult at the moment.

'Mr Forster was complaining of feeling sick,' she replied in the coolest possible tone.

Quite frankly, Sean wouldn't have thought her capable of sounding so frosty and blinked in surprise. Molly had always been known for her warmth, for her kindness, for her sheer *joie de vivre*. Her earlier anger had been upsetting enough but to hear her sounding so frigid was even worse. It sent a shiver straight through his heart. Had he done this to her? Had he turned her from the warm, loving woman he remembered to this… this chilly replica of herself? Even though he hated the idea, he couldn't dismiss it.

'I imagine it's the morphine,' he said evenly, clamping down on the guilt that threatened to swamp him as he lifted the patient's notes out of their holder. Frank Forster had been admitted after complaining of severe pain in his lower back. Apparently, he had been lifting a large Christmas tree off the roof of his car when it had happened. A subsequent scan had shown that one of the discs in his lumbar spine had prolapsed and was pressing on a nerve. The poor man was in a great deal of pain, which was why he had been given morphine while they waited for a bed to become vacant in the spinal unit. Now Sean frowned as he looked up.

'Why didn't Dr Collins prescribe an anti-emetic with the morphine?'

'I have no idea,' Molly replied coldly. She finished straightening the blanket and patted the middle-aged man's hand. 'I'll be back in a moment with something to stop you feeling so sick, Frank. Just hang in there.'

She treated the man to a warm smile and Sean felt some of his guilt ooze away. So the old Molly hadn't disappeared completely, as he had feared. It was just with him that she was so frosty; she was perfectly fine with everyone else. That thought might have set off another round of soul-searching if he had let it, only he refused to do so. As he followed her out of the cubicle, he ruthlessly shoved all those pesky feelings back into their box and slammed the lid. He had to focus on the fact that he had done what he had needed to do to protect her, and that he would do exactly the same thing all over again too if it became necessary…

Wouldn't he?

Sean felt his vision blur, the sterile white walls that surrounded him turning a fuzzy shade of grey. He would finish with Molly again if he had to—of course he would! However, no matter how many times he told himself that, he didn't quite believe it. Maybe he was ninety-nine per cent certain but there was that one per cent of doubt lurking in his mind. One tiny but highly dangerous percentage of uncertainty that sent a chill rippling down his spine. Until he could erase it completely then he couldn't be sure exactly how he would react, so help him!

Molly made her way to the desk, trying to ignore the fact that Sean was following her. That was the best way to handle this situation, she reminded herself— she would ignore him and concentrate on doing her job. It shouldn't be that difficult. They were always so busy that there was little time to think about anything of a personal nature; however, she had to admit that several times she had found her thoughts wandering. Sean had had a major impact on her life and it wasn't easy to forget that when they had been thrust together again like this.

Molly's generous mouth tightened as she set about making the adjustment to Frank Forster's meds. Although she knew exactly what was needed to make the man comfortable, it required a doctor's signature on the prescription. She glanced round, hoping to catch sight of Steph Collins, their F1 student, but there was no sign of her. Although everything was calming down now, there were still a few patients in the unit. Undoubtedly, Steph was dealing with one of them.

'Here. I'll sign that.'

A large tanned hand reached over her shoulder and took the script from her and Molly jumped. She hadn't realised that Sean was standing quite so close to her and she couldn't stop herself reacting. There was a tiny pause and she held her breath as she willed him not to say anything. She didn't want him to suspect how nervous she felt around him, didn't want to admit it to herself even. She just wanted to be indifferent to his presence, as he was undoubtedly indifferent to hers.

The soft rustle of paper as he scrawled his name at the bottom of the script broke the spell. Molly nodded as he handed it back to her without comment, relieved that she had got off so lightly. She would be wary of that happening again, she thought as she took the keys to the drugs cupboard out of her pocket. The last thing she wanted was to appear vulnerable when Sean was around.

'Thanks. I'll get Mr Forster sorted out and then check if there's a bed available yet. He may have to be transferred to Men's Surgical if the Spinal Unit can't come up with anything soon.'

'Hardly ideal, is it, to shunt seriously injured patients about?' Sean observed.

'No. It isn't.' She shrugged, causing another wayward curl to spring out of its clip. 'However, needs must. We either move him to Men's Surgical or get a rocket off the powers-that-be for overrunning the time limit. I sometimes wish that they all had to do a stint down here. Then they might appreciate just how difficult it is to get a patient seen and treated within such a ridiculously short space of time.'

'Amen to that,' Sean murmured. Leaning forward,

he carefully tucked the unruly curl behind her ear and nodded. 'There you go. All nice and tidy again.'

'I...erm...I'll get that anti-emetic.'

Molly turned and fled, uncaring what he thought as she hurried into the office. She could feel her heart pounding in her chest, rapid little flurries that sent the blood gushing through her veins in a red-hot torrent, and bit her lip. She didn't want to react this way, but she couldn't seem to help it. The moment Sean had touched her, it had been as though a fire had reignited inside her and the thought filled her with dismay.

She couldn't go through what she had been through two years ago all over again. Sean had meant the world to her back then; she had honestly thought that she had found her Mr Right, but she had been mistaken. Sean wasn't interested in making a commitment to her or to any woman.

'About what happened before, Molly, well, I'd hate to think that it might create a problem between us.'

Molly spun round so fast when she heard Sean's voice that the room started to whirl around her and she grabbed hold of the desk to steady herself. 'What happened before,' she repeated uncertainly. Her heart suddenly leapt into her throat. Was Sean talking about their affair? Was he attempting to explain why he had ended it so abruptly? Even though it shouldn't have made a scrap of difference now, she found herself holding her breath.

'Yes. That incident with the drunk, I mean.' He grimaced. 'You were quite right to take me to task because I should never have interfered. I've always had the greatest respect for the way you handle even the most difficult patients and I should have left it to you to sort things out.'

'I…' Molly found herself floundering and desperately tried to collect herself. Of course Sean wasn't talking about their affair! That was over and done with so far as he was concerned. In fact, he probably hadn't given her another thought after he had left Dalverston. The idea was so painful that it cut through the muddle in her head as nothing else could have done.

'No, you shouldn't have intervened,' she said flatly, afraid that he would guess how hurt she felt. She drew herself up, forcing all the injured feelings to the deepest, darkest corner of her mind. Letting herself get upset at this stage was pointless. It wouldn't change what had happened; neither would she want it to. 'I was perfectly capable of handling it myself. However, there seems little point going on and on about it. It's all over and done with now.'

'Of course. I just wouldn't want it to cause any…well, friction between us. I realise that working together isn't exactly ideal but I'm hoping that we can call a truce. Do you think that's possible, Molly? Can we put what happened two years ago behind us?'

'It isn't an issue,' she said quickly and then flushed when she saw the scepticism in his eyes. 'Don't flatter

yourself, Sean. Oh, I may have been upset at the time—
I'll admit it. However, I soon got over it, I assure you.'

'Good. I'm pleased to hear it.' He grinned at her, apparently relieved to have got everything settled so successfully. 'Right, I'd better get back before we have a
mutiny on our hands. The rest of the team will think
we've gone AWOL!'

Molly filled in the sheet to say that she had taken
the prescribed drugs after he had left then took a deep
breath before she made her way back to the unit. From
this point on she would follow Sean's example and treat
him as nothing more than a colleague. It was only what
he was, in all honesty, so it shouldn't be that difficult,
especially after what he had said to her just now.

A tiny stab of pain speared through her heart but she
steadfastly ignored it. Obviously, Sean didn't view her
as anything more than someone he worked with and
she was glad about that too!

CHAPTER THREE

IT WAS WELL after seven a.m. before Sean finally left the unit. Although he had been due to leave at six there had been a last-minute rush which had held everyone up, not that he minded. As he made his way to the staff car park, he deliberately set about erasing the night's events from his mind. There was no point dwelling on what Molly had said about how quickly she had got over him. And definitely no point wondering why he had felt so hurt when he had heard it. He had learned through experience that it was best not to examine his feelings in too much depth. No, they had called a truce and that was it. End of story.

Sean sighed as he unlocked his car and got in, all too aware how shallow it made him appear to take such a view. However, as he couldn't think of a better approach, he had to go along with it. There was a film of ice covering the windscreen and he switched on the engine to clear it. There were a lot of night staff leaving at the same time and he recognised several people from the last time he had worked at Dalverston.

He had enjoyed his stint here, he mused as he waited for the ice to melt. There was a strong community feel about the hospital, plus it was situated in such a glorious part of the country. He knew that they were desperately in need of a permanent registrar to fill the vacancy in A&E and was seriously tempted to apply for the post himself. He would enjoy living and working here full-time.

The thought shocked him, mainly because it was the first time that he had seriously considered taking a permanent post. After Claire had died so tragically in that road accident, he had found it impossible to settle. He had signed on with a leading medical agency and taken only short-term contracts ever since. Two months here, six months there; it had been exactly what he had wanted. To suddenly discover that his peripatetic lifestyle had started to pall was a shock and not a pleasant one either, especially when it was the thought of working here that had triggered it. It would be asking for trouble if he remained in Dalverston. Working with Molly, day in and day out, would be far too much for him to handle.

As though thinking about her had somehow conjured her up, Molly suddenly appeared. Sean felt his heart and what felt like the rest of his vital organs scrunch up inside him as he watched her walk over to her car. She had parked in the row behind him and he studied her reflection in his rear-view mirror. She looked weary, only to be expected after the busy night they'd had, but was that the only reason for the defeated slump to her shoulders? Or had it anything to do with him? Had she found it a strain to work with him after what had happened between them in the past? Even though there was little he could do about it, he hated to think that *he* was the cause of her unhappiness. Out of all the women he had dated since Claire had died, Molly was the only one he had truly cared about.

Molly slid the key into the lock and opened the car door. Picking up the can of de-icer, she squirted a generous dollop onto the frosty windscreen. She hated winter, hated the fact that she couldn't just get in her car and drive away. There was no point pretending—working with Sean had been an ordeal, one she wished with every scrap of her being that she wouldn't have to repeat, but there was no hope of that, was there? He was covering the entire Christmas and New Year period which meant he would be around for at least six weeks and probably longer if the management team could persuade him to stay on. Finding cover over the festive period was always difficult as most locums wanted to be with their families at this time of the year. There were very few with Sean's skills and experience willing to relocate.

Molly tucked the can under the passenger seat, trying not to think about the problems it could cause if she had to see Sean on a daily basis. Slipping the key into the ignition, she attempted to start the engine, only to be rewarded by a nasty grunting noise. She tried again with the same result. The battery, always dodgy, was completely flat. Brilliant! Now she would have to catch the bus, which was just what she needed after the night she'd had.

'Problems?'

Molly almost jumped out of her skin when her car door opened. She had no idea where Sean had appeared from and found it impossible to reply. He gave her a quick smile as leant into the car to try starting the engine himself.

'Sounds like a flat battery to me,' he declared when he received the same response. Resting his forearm against the roof of the car, he grinned down at her. 'They always go at the worst possible moment, don't they?'

It was the sort of comment anyone might have made in such circumstances, so Molly had no idea why she reacted as she did. 'Thank you, but I did manage to work that out for myself! Now, if you'll move aside...'

She gave the door a hefty push to fully open it, not even flinching when it caught him a glancing blow on his hip. It was his own fault for poking his nose in again where it wasn't wanted, she assured herself as she lifted her bag off the passenger seat. She didn't need his help. She didn't want anything to do with him. Quite frankly, if he disappeared in a puff of smoke it would make her day!

Slamming the car door, she started walking towards

the gate, wondering how long it would be before a bus came along. She lived on the other side of the town and it took forever by bus, which was why she had saved up for a car.

She was just nearing the gate when she saw her bus coming along the road and started to run, but it was difficult to make much progress thanks to the frosty conditions underfoot. She groaned as she was forced to watch it drive away. She would have to wait at least half an hour before another came along.

'Hop in. I'll give you a lift.' Sean drew up beside her but Molly shook her head.

'No, thank you. I prefer to wait for the next bus,' she said snippily.

'Are you sure?' He shrugged, his broad shoulders moving lightly beneath his heavy quilted jacket, and Molly gulped. Sean had always possessed the most wonderful physique and it seemed little had changed in that respect. He had gone running when they had been seeing each other, setting off early each morning so he could fit in a run before work.

How many times had he come back from one of those runs and persuaded her to take a shower with him? she wondered suddenly. She had no idea but the memory of those times seemed to flood her mind. They had made love in the shower, their desire heightened by the sensuous feel of the hot water cascading over their naked bodies, and then followed it up by making love all over again in her bed. She had never realised that lovemaking could feel like that, had never experienced desire on such a level before. It was Sean who had taught her what it could be like. Only Sean who could make her feel that way again too.

The thought was too much. It made a mockery of all the plans she had made about how she intended to live her life in the future. What hope did she have of sticking to her decision to be in charge of her own destiny when one night working with Sean had had this effect? She had to rid herself of all these foolish memories, finally put an end to that episode in her life. Until she did so she would be always looking back, constantly comparing how she felt now to how she had felt then.

It was the way she should set about it that was the big question—how to totally and completely erase Sean Fitzgerald from her consciousness. Oh, she had tried her best over the past couple of years and thought she had succeeded too, but obviously not. He was still there in her head, a spectre from her past who refused to budge, and until she rid herself of him then she would never be free to move on. Maybe it had been a mistake to try to blot him out of her mind, to try and forget the heartache he had caused her. Maybe she needed to face up to it, to face up to *him*?

It was Sean who had called the shots in the past, Sean who had ended their affair too, but maybe she needed to take charge this time—instigate another affair with him and bring it to a conclusion when *she* decided the time was right. One of the worst things about the whole unhappy experience was the effect it had had on her self-confidence. She'd been left feeling used, feeling like a victim, and she wasn't prepared to put up with feeling that way any more. This time neither her life nor her heart would be left in tatters. This time she would make sure of that!

'So what's it to be then? Are you going to wait for the next bus—a long and undoubtedly chilly wait—or are you going to accept my offer of a lift? I mean we did agree to call a truce, so what's the problem?'

Sean dredged up a deliberately taunting smile although it wasn't easy, he had to admit. There was just something about the expression on Molly's face that had set all his internal alarm bells ringing. He had seen that kind of expression before on other women's faces and had learned to tread warily until he discovered its cause. Whilst he had no idea what Molly was planning, instinct warned him that he wasn't going to like it.

'There isn't a problem. Why not, if you're going my way?'

Molly walked round to the passenger's side and got in, leaving Sean suddenly wishing that he had never made the offer in the first place. The less time he spent with Molly, the better, quite frankly, but he could hardly renege on his offer now. He slid the car into gear and drove out of the gates, his mind racing this way and that. Was Molly plotting something, some sort of payback perhaps for the way he had treated her? It wouldn't be the first time it had happened, although fortunately he had managed to deflect the woman's ire before it had caused too much damage. However, if that was what Molly was planning then it might not be as easy to resolve the problem this time. The difference was that he *cared* about Molly and would hate to do anything that might hurt her even more.

They drove through the centre of the town in silence. Sean was so caught up in wondering what Molly might be planning to do that he found it impossible to make small-talk as he normally would have done. She lived in a tiny terraced cottage close to the river and he drew up outside with a feeling of relief. If she really was looking to pay him back then the best solution was to steer well clear of her. Fair enough, they would still have to work together, but outside of work he would make sure he kept his distance. It was only what he had intended to do after all—stay away from her—so it was surprising how much the idea stung.

'Right. Here you are. I bet you're looking forward to getting to bed. I know I am.'

It was meant to be an off-the-cuff remark, a throwaway comment free from any significance. However, the second the words were out of his mouth, Sean regretted them. Why in heaven's name had he mentioned *bed*? Stirring up those kinds of memories was the *last* thing he should be doing!

'Hmm. It's always good to snuggle down in a nice warm bed after working nights, isn't it?' Molly replied in a tone he had never heard her use before.

Sean felt the hair all over his body spring to attention and then salute. Felt other bits of him follow suit and almost groaned out loud in dismay. When had Molly perfected the art of sounding so…so *seductive*? Two years ago he would have described her as the girl-next-door: sweet, warm, loving and giving. Now she sounded more like a siren and, worst of all, he was responding to her call! Panic overwhelmed him at that point. It made no difference that he was highly experienced in the ways of women; it still took a massive effort of will to control his baser urges.

'It is.' He dredged up a smile, not wanting her to guess how he really felt in case it gave her an advantage. Quite frankly, it seemed to him that she was already holding all the aces. If he didn't want to end up with the losing hand, then he needed to be extremely careful how he played this game. 'Right, I'd better be off then. I hope you manage to get your car sorted out.'

'I hope so too.' She leant towards him as she unfastened her seat belt and he inwardly shuddered when he felt the warmth of her breath caress his cheek. 'Thanks for the lift, Sean. I really appreciate it. Can I tempt you to come in for a cup of coffee as a thank you, perhaps?'

Her green eyes stared straight into his and Sean felt his resolve start to crumble away when he saw the invitation they held. It was obvious that coffee wasn't the only thing on her mind.

'Thanks but I'd better get straight off home,' he mumbled, praying that he would manage to hold out

long enough to make his excuses and leave, as the tab-
loid journalists were so fond of saying. 'There's a couple of things I need to do this afternoon, so the sooner
I get to sleep the better.'

'Pity. Still, there's always another time.' She gave
him a lingering smile then opened the car door.

Sean gripped tight hold of the steering wheel as she
climbed out, knowing that if he let go he would regret it.
He wouldn't follow her inside the house, he told himself
sternly, not on any pretext. Not when he felt this way.
He made himself sit there and wait while she unlocked
the front door, even managed to wave before he drove
away, but his heart was going nineteen to the dozen.
He had a very good idea what Molly was plotting, what
form her retribution would take. She was planning to
seduce him and, once he was under her spell, then undoubtedly she would ditch him exactly as he had done
to her. Quite frankly, he wasn't sure what shocked him
most, the fact that sweet, *gentle* Molly should come up
with such a plan, or how much the idea terrified him.

After all, now he knew what was afoot, he could take
steps to prevent it happening, couldn't he? He could
resist her overtures and stick to being a colleague and
nothing more. It should be easy-peasy but he knew in
his heart that it wouldn't be. The problem was that he
wasn't sure if he could resist if Molly tried to lure him
back into her bed. Even though he might know why
she was doing it, would it be enough to put him off? Or
would the thought of holding her in his arms and ex-

periencing everything he had felt two years ago prove too much?

Sean groaned as he drew up at the traffic lights when they changed to red. Logically, the fact that Molly was simply trying to pay him back for what he had done to her should have been enough to guarantee that he would refuse to get involved with her again. However, it wasn't his head that was dictating his actions this time but his heart, and his heart was playing by its own rules. There was no guarantee that he could hold out if Molly was determined to get her own way. Absolutely no guarantee at all.

CHAPTER FOUR

MOLLY COULD SCARCELY believe what she had just done. As she made her way into the kitchen and flopped down onto a chair, she could feel her heart thumping. She had just—quite blatantly too—tried to seduce Sean!

She took a deep breath and made herself hold it for the count of ten, but it didn't help. Her nerves were fizzing, her heart racing, and other bits of her—well, she couldn't begin to describe what they were doing. Never in all of her twenty-seven years had she done such a thing. All right, so maybe she had decided to be more proactive in her approach to any future relationships, but it was one thing to think about it and another entirely to put it into practice. If Sean had come in for coffee then would she have gone through with it and invited him into her bed as well?

She shot to her feet, unable to deal with the thought or the one that followed it. Had Sean guessed what she was planning and was that why he had been so eager to leave? After all, it wasn't the first time he had rejected her, was it? Sean had made it perfectly clear two years ago that he wasn't interested in her and yet she had still gone ahead with her crazy scheme. He was probably laughing his head off at her pathetic attempt to seduce him!

Molly groaned out loud, feeling completely humiliated. How could she face him again after this? She would have to try to change her shifts and avoid working with him, although it wouldn't be easy to do so. The Christmas and New Year rosters had been prepared weeks ago and making changes at this late stage would create far too many problems. No, she couldn't see it happening, which meant she would just have to grit her teeth and get on with it. All she could do was pray that he wouldn't mention what had happened that morning. She honestly didn't think she could cope with being subjected to any of his teasing remarks or, worse still, becoming the object of his pity.

It was all very depressing. Molly's spirits were at an all-time low as she heated some milk in the microwave and made herself a cup of hot chocolate, hoping it would soothe her rattled nerves enough so that she could sleep. However, after an hour spent tossing and turning in her bed, she gave up. How could she sleep with all these thoughts milling around inside her head?

She went into the sitting room and curled up on the sofa, telling herself that it was silly to panic. After all, nothing had happened, had it? Even if Sean had guessed what she had been planning to do, there was still time to change her mind. Quite honestly, it wasn't worth it if it caused this kind of upset; she would be stupid to go ahead... And yet there was still that niggling little thought at the back of her mind that she would never be entirely free of him until she had brought their relationship to a conclusion in her own time and in her own way too.

Molly closed her eyes, trying to imagine how she would feel afterwards. Elated, possibly? Relieved, hopefully? People continually trotted out that well-worn phrase about finding closure, so was that what would happen? Would it bring things to a nice tidy finale if she slept with Sean and subsequently dumped him?

She tried her best to imagine how she would feel but it was impossible to see into the future. She could only go by how she was feeling at this very moment—confused, embarrassed, scared. What if she followed through with her plan and it backfired on her? What if she slept with Sean only to find that she had fallen under his spell once again? That would only make matters even worse.

Her thoughts spun round and round in circles until she felt positively giddy. She knew that it was pointless going back to bed as she would never be able to sleep. She showered and dressed then left the house, hoping that a walk would help to calm her. She took the path leading to the river, carefully picking her way around the icy puddles. The river looked sluggish this morning, a skin of ice coating its surface. There were some ducks slipping and sliding their way across the ice and she stopped to watch them for a moment before the biting cold drove her on. When she came to the path leading up to the town centre, she hesitated, wondering if she should treat herself to coffee and a croissant before she went home. She hadn't had anything to eat since she'd got back from work and her stomach was rumbling.

Molly followed the path and soon arrived at the market square. The council had erected a huge Christmas tree in the centre of it and she stopped to admire it. There was a group of carol singers from one of the local churches gathered around it and she listened as they sang several well-known carols. It was all very festive and so very normal that she started to relax. There was no point getting het up. The choice was hers. She could either put her plan into action or forget about it.

'All very Christmassy, isn't it? I love hearing Christmas carols at this time of the year, don't you?'

Molly spun round, feeling her heart leap into her throat when she found Sean standing beside her. 'What are you doing here?' she snapped, unable to hide her dismay. That he should turn up just when she was starting to get her thoughts together was too much.

'Same as you, I imagine. Enjoying the singing.'

He gave her a quick smile then dug into his pocket and dropped a handful of change into the bucket when a child approached them, looking for donations, and the fact that he didn't even bother to check how much he had given struck a chord in Molly's memory. Sean had always been incredibly generous, the first to donate whenever anyone was raising money for a good cause. It was one of the things she had admired most about him, in fact, his unstinting generosity.

It was such a small thing yet it had a profound effect on her. Somewhere along the way, she had forgotten all the things she had liked about him. The pain of his leaving had negated everything else yet all of a sudden it all came rushing back: his generosity, his kindness, his compassion for those less fortunate than himself. Sean had possessed so many good qualities, so many things to commend him that she found herself wondering all of a sudden why he had behaved so out of character towards her. Sean cared about people, genuinely cared, so why had he been so cruel when he had ended their relationship?

'How about that cup of coffee you mentioned earlier?'

Molly jumped when he touched her lightly on the arm. She'd been so lost in her thoughts that she had no idea what he had said. 'Pardon?'

'Coffee.' He smiled down at her, his blue eyes filled with laughter and another emotion that she had never expected to see again. Did he really care about her, or was he merely a highly accomplished actor? She had no idea and before she could attempt to work it out he slid his hand under her elbow. 'I fancy a coffee and a croissant so will you join me, Molly? I think we deserve a treat after the busy night we had, don't you?'

He briskly led her across the pavement to the café

before she had a chance to reply, opening the café door with a flourish that set the brass bell jingling. Molly took a deep breath as she stepped inside, drinking in the scent of coffee and warm pastries. Her senses seemed to be ridiculously heightened all of a sudden so that the familiar aromas seemed richer and more enticing than ever. Even the colours of the checked tablecloths seemed brighter, the reds and blues and greens dazzling her eyes. It was as though she had stepped out of the gloom into full, glorious daylight and it was the strangest experience.

'Oh, look. That couple's leaving. Go and grab their table while I order our coffee.'

Sean gave her a little push towards the newly vacant table and Molly obediently headed in that direction. She sat down, automatically unwinding her scarf and removing her woolly hat. What was going on? Why did she feel this way, as though she had suddenly woken from a deep sleep?

'Here we go. They'll fetch our coffee over in a moment. I ordered you a latte. I hope that was OK. It used to be your favourite, if I remember correctly.'

Sean had reappeared with a tray heaped with warm croissants and miniature pots of jam and Molly jumped. She could feel her pulse popping as she watched him unload everything onto the table, croissants and jam, napkins and knives. He was quick and deft, his hands soon setting everything to rights, but that was his way. Whatever Sean did, he did it well. From work to something as mundane as setting a table, he gave it his all. That was why it had been such a pleasure to be with him. Everything appeared more interesting, more *vibrant* when Sean was around.

Even her.

Molly took a croissant off the plate and bit into it, savouring its buttery richness. It had been ages since anything had tasted so good, two years in fact. Two long years, during which time she had lived her life in the shadows. Now Sean was back, everything had changed. Now she felt completely and fully alive. And it simply proved just how desperately she needed to break his hold over her.

'Thanks.'

Sean smiled as the waitress placed their coffees on the table. He saw the interest in the girl's eyes as she smiled back at him but he ignored it. At any other time he might have been tempted to follow up on it and ask her out on a date. It was something he had done more times than he could count over the years, but he wasn't even tempted. Not when he was with Molly. He simply wasn't interested in other women when he was with her. He never had been.

It was a sobering thought, doubly so when it was the first time he had admitted it. When he and Molly had been seeing one another, he hadn't looked at another woman. She had filled his thoughts to the exclusion of anyone else. Was that why he had ended their affair so abruptly? he wondered. Because he had realised on some inner level that he was getting far too involved with her? At the time he had told himself that he was doing it for her sake, that he was taking steps to protect her, but had his decision been less altruistic than he had thought? Had he been trying to protect himself as much as her?

It was an unsettling thought and one that Sean knew he was going to have to think about. He couldn't just brush it under the carpet as he normally would do—that wouldn't work. He needed to examine his feelings, face up to how he had felt two years ago, and take whatever action was necessary to ensure it didn't happen again. The problem was that he had put Molly on a bit of a pedestal, painted her in his mind as the ideal woman, and it was time he stopped doing that. Maybe Molly's plan wasn't so way off-beam as he had thought. If they resumed their affair, it could help *him* put things into perspective.

It was something else that Sean knew he needed to think about, but not right now. He helped himself to a croissant, murmuring appreciatively as he bit into it. 'This is delicious! No wonder the place is packed, although I don't remember the food being this good when I ate here before.'

'The café changed hands last year and, apparently, the new owner is French and only uses French milled flour for his croissants and pastries,' Molly informed him, wiping her buttery fingers on a paper napkin.

'Really? Well, good for him. It's obviously paying dividends.'

Sean grinned at her, thinking how pretty she looked that day. She was wearing a pale pink sweater and jeans and she looked so young and so fresh as she sat there, enjoying her breakfast, that it was little wonder that he had always loved being with her. And it was that thought which helped to unleash all sorts of memories he had thought he had buried.

'Remember those croissants we used to buy from the supermarket?' he said reminiscently. 'We used to heat them in the microwave so they were always slightly soggy yet we still ate them.'

'Yes, I remember,' Molly said quietly, wishing that he hadn't brought up the subject. It had become a sort of ritual for them—if their days off had coincided then Sean would make coffee for them while she warmed up the croissants and then they would take everything back to bed. More often than not the coffee would grow cold because once they were under the covers the inevitable would happen...

'We didn't always get to eat them, though, did we, Molly?'

His tone was brooding and she knew that he was remembering what had happened, how their desire for each other had overruled everything else. Sean had wanted her just as much as she had wanted him, which made his subsequent actions all the more difficult to understand. All of a sudden, Molly realised that she needed to know what had gone wrong, why he had ended their affair so abruptly and with so little warning.

'What happened, Sean? What went wrong?'

'I'm sorry?'

A frown furrowed his brow as he looked at her and Molly almost weakened. After all, what was the point of asking questions like that now? It wouldn't change what had happened—nothing would. And yet there was still this need to know why he had behaved the way he had. Even allowing for the fact that Sean had made it clear that he didn't do commitment, it was strange.

'Something must have happened to make you end our relationship so suddenly, so what was it? Was it something I did?'

'You didn't do anything. I just felt that it was the best thing to do,' he said flatly.

'Best for who?' She gave a brittle little laugh. 'Were you tired of me, Sean—was that it? Did you want someone more exciting in your life?'

'No. It wasn't that.' He reached across the table and touched her hand. 'I was never, ever bored when we were together, Molly. That's the truth. I swear.'

He withdrew his hand and she had a feeling that he was trying to decide what to say. She held her breath, wondering what he was going to tell her, but in the end he merely picked up his cup and drank some of his coffee.

Molly sipped her own coffee, wondering why she felt

so deflated. There was no reason to believe that Sean had some secret he was hiding, yet she couldn't shake off the idea that something in his past had had a huge bearing on his actions. She sighed as she reached for another pastry. It was merely wishful thinking; she was looking for a complicated reason to explain why he had ended their affair when the truth was far simpler. He had tired of her and had wanted a change.

CHAPTER FIVE

SEAN COULDN'T BELIEVE how tempted he'd been to tell Molly all about Claire and the vow he had made. After all, what would it have achieved? It wouldn't have changed anything. On the contrary, it could have made matters worse. Molly might have thought he was aiming for the sympathy vote and he really couldn't bear that.

He reached for a second croissant then stopped when the café door was flung open and a woman came rushing in. Sean immediately leapt to his feet when he saw the panic on her face. He was already heading towards her even before she managed to speak.

'It's my husband! He's collapsed. Can someone help me? Please!'

'Where is he?' Sean took hold of her arm when she swayed. 'I'm a doctor so show me where he is and I'll see what I can do to help.'

'He's over there, by the Christmas tree. We were listening to the carol singers when he suddenly started acting really strange,' the woman explained as she led the way to where a crowd was starting to gather.

'In what way was he acting strange?' Sean asked, pushing his way through the onlookers. Someone had placed the man in the recovery position, so he knelt down beside him and checked his pulse then made sure he was breathing.

'I don't know…he couldn't seem to speak properly 'cos his mouth was drooping at one side and he couldn't move his left arm either.' The middle-aged woman bit back a sob. 'I tried to get him to tell me what was wrong but it was as though he couldn't hear me and then all of a sudden he just fell down onto the ground and didn't move.'

'I see,' Sean said quietly. It sounded very much like a stroke to him and the sooner the man was moved to hospital the better his chances would be. He looked up when Molly came to join them, nodding when she told him that she had phoned for an ambulance. 'Thanks. Can you get back onto Ambulance Control and tell them it looks like a stroke? That way, everyone will be pre-pared when he arrives at A&E.'

'Of course.' She swiftly made the call then knelt down beside him. 'How's his breathing?'

'So far, so good. Pulse is a bit erratic, but that's only to be expected.' He glanced up at the man's wife. 'Did he complain of a headache shortly before it happened?'

'No. He seemed perfectly fine. We were just going to listen to another couple of carols and then go and have a drink in the café before we went home,' the poor woman replied. 'Why did you ask that? Do you know what's wrong with him?'

'I'm afraid it looks very much like he's had a stroke,' Sean explained gently, knowing it would be a shock for her.

'A stroke,' she repeated. Tears rushed to her eyes. 'Is…is he going to die?'

Molly stood up and put her arm around her. 'Let's not assume the worst,' she told her quietly. 'The main thing now is to get your husband to hospital so he can receive treatment.'

'Can you treat him, though? My dad had a stroke when I was a teenager and there was nothing anyone could do…'

She broke off, too upset to continue, and Sean sighed. This was a part of his job he hated, trying to reassure relatives while not making any promises he might not be able to keep.

'We've made a lot of advances in the way we treat stroke patients in recent years. Your husband will be given anticoagulants to break down any clots that may have formed in his brain. It's a treatment that can have very positive results.'

'What if it's a burst blood vessel, though? That's what happened to my dad—a blood vessel burst and caused a massive bleed in his brain.'

'Your husband will have a CT scan at the hospital to rule that out. However, the fact that he didn't complain of a severe headache would point towards it being a clot rather than a bleed,' Sean explained.

He looked up when the wail of a siren announced the arrival of the ambulance. Molly was still talking to the woman, doing her best to reassure her, so Sean left her to it while he did the hand-over. It didn't take long as he hadn't administered any form of treatment so within minutes the ambulance was on its way. Molly sighed as she watched it drive off.

'Think he'll make it?'

'He stands a pretty good chance,' Sean replied quietly. 'Prompt treatment can make a huge difference in a case like this and that's what he will receive.'

'Yes, you're right. His poor wife, though. It must be a terrible shock when something like that happens to someone you love.'

'Your life changes in an instant,' Sean agreed, knowing only too well how that felt. Loving someone made you vulnerable and it was a timely reminder that he needed to get a grip on his emotions. He couldn't go through that kind of heartache a second time, which was why he needed to keep his distance from Molly.

It was a sobering thought. As Sean followed her back into the café, he realised that he needed to forget any ideas he had harboured about them resuming their affair. Although it might resolve certain issues, what if it created a whole lot more? Even though it wasn't easy to admit it, he had been far more involved with her than he had thought, and it was scary to wonder what might happen in the future if they grew close again.

'I'd better get off home. Thanks for the coffee.'

Molly pulled on her hat then wound her scarf around her neck in readiness to leave and Sean was suddenly struck by an inexplicable need to explain why he had ended their relationship two years ago. Would it help if he told her the real reason why he could never commit himself? he wondered. Once Molly understood then maybe they could both move on; she could put it all behind her and he could stop thinking about how he had felt when they had been together. The last thing he wanted was Molly going ahead with her plan to seduce him—that would be a complete and utter disaster!

'There's something I should have told you ages ago,' he said hurriedly.

'I really can't see the point of dragging up the past at this stage, Sean.' She looked up and her expression was so distant that he fell silent. She gave him a tight little smile as she picked up her gloves. 'If it was that important then you should have told me before now. It's really none of my business now, is it? We're not together any more.'

She was right; there was no point in baring his soul after all this time. He was only going to be in Dalverston for a few more weeks and after that he would make sure that he never came back here again. No, the time for confessions was long gone and he would be foolish to imagine it would make any difference if he told her the truth.

'You're right. It's all water under the bridge, isn't it?' He treated her to a deliberately bright smile. 'I think I'll have another coffee before I head off home. I'll see you tonight, I expect.'

'I expect so.'

She matched his smile, wattage for wattage, then headed for the door. Sean went to the counter and ordered himself a double espresso, hoping that a serious shot of caffeine would help to get him back on track. He was allowing his emotions to get the better of him, something he never did, and he had to stop.

He sighed as he took his coffee back to the table and sat down. It was being around Molly that was causing him to behave so out of character. It had been exactly the same two years ago—he had known that he and Molly could never have a long-term relationship, yet he had put off breaking up with her until it had been almost too late. She had the strangest effect on him, made him long for things he knew he could never have, but he was going to stand firm, no matter what.

He took a sip of coffee, shuddering as the caffeine hit his central nervous system. It might be tempting but being back in Molly's arms was something he intended to avoid at all costs.

CHAPTER SIX

MOLLY FELT EXHAUSTED when she arrived at work that night. The lack of sleep combined with everything else that had happened recently had taken their toll and her energy levels were at an all-time low. It was all she could do to dredge up a smile when she found Suzy in the staffroom.

'You look absolutely shattered!' Suzy exclaimed. She put her hands on her hips and glared at Molly. 'I hope it hasn't anything to do with Sean Fitzgerald. You had a bit of thing for him the last time he worked here, didn't you?'

'All water under the bridge,' Molly declared, groaning when she unwittingly repeated the phrase Sean had used only that morning. It shouldn't have been a surprise. After all, she had spent most of the day thinking about him. Had he been going to share some sort of a confidence with her? she wondered for the umpteenth time, and sighed. Even if he had, he had soon thought better of it. No, Sean wasn't about to share any confidences with *her*. She wasn't that important to him.

She brushed aside that depressing thought. 'You know what they say, Suzy. You have to kiss a lot of frogs before you find a real live prince.'

'And that's honestly how you view him, is it?' Suzy retorted. 'As just another frog?'

'Well, he certainly hasn't turned into a prince,' Molly stated.

She swept out of the door before Suzy could reply, knowing that she wasn't up to having a discussion about this particular frog prince. Although Suzy knew that she had dated Sean when he had last worked there, her friend had no idea how Molly had really felt about him. After all, everyone in the hospital knew that Sean didn't do commitment so there was no reason why Suzy should have guessed that she had fallen so heavily for him and that was how she wanted it to remain. It was bad enough knowing what a fool she had been without everyone else knowing it too.

Molly did the handover then took her first patient to Cubicles. Abbey Jones was suffering from severe stomach cramps which she thought were the result of a curry she had eaten that lunchtime. Her boyfriend had brought her into hospital but Molly asked him to remain in the waiting room while she got Abbey settled. She needed to ask Abbey some questions and she preferred to do so in private as it didn't sound to her as though Abbey was suffering from food poisoning.

'Have you been sick?' Molly asked once she had made Abbey comfortable on the bed.

'No. It's just these pains in my stomach.' Abbey drew up her legs and moaned. 'It really hurts!'

'The doctor will be here to see you in a minute,' Molly said soothingly. 'Let's get these leggings off you for starters.' She helped the girl remove her boots and leggings, trying to hide her dismay when she discovered that Abbey was bleeding from the vagina. 'Did you know that you were bleeding?'

'No! I knew I felt a bit damp down there but I slipped over in the car park on my way in and landed in a puddle so I thought it must be that. What's happening to me, Sister?'

'Is it possible that you might be pregnant?' Molly said carefully.

'Pregnant,' Abbey repeated, looking stunned.

'Yes. Can you remember when you last had a period?' Molly persisted.

'I'm not sure… I've always been very irregular, you see. Sometimes I can go five or six weeks between periods so it's difficult to say for certain.' Abbey gulped. 'If I am pregnant then why am I bleeding like this? Am I having a miscarriage or something?'

'It's possible.' Molly patted her hand, knowing what a shock it must be for her. Not to have realised that she was pregnant and then have this happen would be a lot for any woman to deal with. After she had split from Sean, she'd had a worrying few days herself when her period had been late, even though they had been meticulous about using protection. Thankfully, everything had resolved itself although she couldn't help wondering what she would have done if she had been pregnant. Would she have contacted Sean and told him about the baby? She wasn't sure. After all, he had made it abundantly clear that he hadn't wanted anything more to do with her, hadn't he?

Molly pushed aside that thought as she focused on finding out if Abbey was indeed pregnant. She fetched a pregnancy testing kit from the cupboard and helped her to the bathroom. When Abbey reappeared a few minutes later, she was shaking.

'It's positive,' she whispered. 'I had no idea I was pregnant and now it looks as though I'm going to lose the baby.'

'I'm so sorry,' Molly said gently as she helped her back onto the bed. 'It must be a terrible shock for you, but the main thing now is to get you sorted out. Do you want me to tell your boyfriend or would you rather do it yourself? It's entirely up to you.'

'I don't know!' Tears began to pour down Abbey's cheeks. 'We've only been going out for a couple of months and we've never even spoken about having kids. I really don't know what I should do for the best.'

'You don't have to decide right this very minute,' Molly assured her, understanding only too well what a dilemma it must be for the girl. She and Sean had never discussed having children either, for obvious reasons, i.e. he'd had no intention of committing himself for the long-term. A child would have caused an unwelcome disruption to his plans, and the thought hurt even though she knew how stupid it was to let it affect her.

'I'll just tell him that you're being transferred to a ward for further tests,' Molly said hurriedly, not wanting to go any further down that route.

'Yes. Thank you.' Abbey wiped her eyes. 'It's such a lot to take in.'

'It must be.'

Molly treated her to a smile then went to the desk and phoned the maternity unit. Sean appeared as she was ending the call and she quickly explained what was happening.

'Sounds as though you've sorted everything out.' He frowned. 'Who brought her in?'

'Her boyfriend.' Molly nodded towards the waiting room. 'He's over there. I had a feeling that it wasn't food poisoning and asked him to remain out here while I examined Abbey.'

'It will be a shock for him too, I imagine,' Sean observed.

'If she chooses to tell him.' Molly smiled tightly, conscious of the dilemma she would have been in if the same thing had happened to her. 'They've only been seeing one another for a few months and she isn't sure if she wants him to know or not.'

'Really?' Sean's tone was grim. Molly frowned because it wasn't how she would have expected him to react. If anything, she would have thought that he would be all in favour of Abbey keeping the news to herself if it meant there would be less pressure put on her boyfriend.

'Yes.' She shrugged. 'Maybe it's a good idea if they're not in a committed relationship.'

'I disagree. Keeping something like this a secret only creates problems, in my opinion. But if it's what the patient wants then we have to go along with it.'

He didn't say anything else as he made his way to Cubicles to see Abbey. Molly wasn't sure what to make of it all as his reaction had been the complete opposite to what she would have expected. Did Sean have personal experience of this kind of situation? she wondered suddenly as she went to speak to Abbey's boyfriend. And was that why he had taken such a hard stance just now? Her mind raced off at a tangent and she gasped. Did it also explain why he avoided commitment? Because he had been so badly hurt at some point in his life that he refused to run the risk of being hurt ever again?

It was an intriguing thought, but Molly knew that she mustn't make the mistake of reading too much into it. To allow herself to believe that it was the true explanation for the way he had treated her two years ago would be asking for trouble. No, the truth was probably much simpler: Sean had grown tired of her and ended their relationship.

By the time everything was sorted out quite a large queue had formed in Reception. Suzy was doing triage that night—making sure the most seriously injured were seen first. Ambulance control had rung as well to say there was a young man who'd been involved in an RTA on his way. He had a suspected fractured pelvis so Molly told the paramedics to take him straight to Resus when he arrived and buzzed for Sean. As the senior doctor on duty, he was the one who would need to deal with this casualty and she would assist him.

'Right, so what's happened here?' Sean hurried into Resus and came straight over to the bed. Molly moved aside to give him some room as he bent over the bed. He was wearing light blue scrubs that night and she found herself thinking all of a sudden just how much the colour suited him, emphasising the intense sapphire-blue of his eyes. Sean was an extremely handsome man, with that jet-black hair and those clean-cut features, and it was impossible to ignore the fact too. It took every scrap of willpower she could muster to concentrate as the lead paramedic did the handover.

'This is David Gregory, aged twenty-two. He came off his motorbike after hitting a pothole in the road and slammed into a stone wall,' the paramedic explained. 'There appears to be some instability around his pelvis which is why we fitted a belt. He's had ten mgs of morphine for the pain plus eight mgs of metoclopramide to counteract any sickness.' The crew finished off with an update of the patient's BP and Sats before they left.

'Hello, David. I'm Dr Fitzgerald. I know you must be in a great deal of pain but I need to check what damage you've done to yourself. OK?'

Sean set about his examination when David nodded. He was quick but thorough, his hands moving as gently as possible over the young man's hips and pelvis. He glanced at Molly and she could see the concern in his eyes. 'Can you organise an X-ray, please, Sister? There's quite a bit of movement here and I'd like to check if we're dealing with more than one fracture.'

'Of course.' Molly hurried to the phone and summoned the radiographer. She arrived just moments later and quickly set about taking the X-rays they needed. Resus was equipped with an overhead X-ray machine so there was no need to move the patient. They all stepped aside while the films were taken and in a very short time the results were up on the screen. As Sean had suspected, David Gregory had fractured his pelvis in not one but two places, which made the situation even more complicated.

'He needs to go to Theatre ASAP,' Sean said after studying the films. 'If I'm not mistaken, there's some damage to the bladder and that needs sorting out immediately. Who's the surgeon on duty tonight—do you know?'

'I think it's Adam Humphreys,' Molly informed him. 'Do you want me to phone him and tell him we have a patient for him?'

'If you wouldn't mind.' Sean smiled at her. 'Thanks, Molly. It will save me a job.'

'No problem.' Molly gave a little shrug before she hurried over to the phone but she couldn't ignore the fact that her heart had lifted when Sean had smiled at her. Was she right about him being hurt in the past? she wondered once again and then sighed. She had to stop trying to find excuses for him and simply accept that he had finished with her because he hadn't wanted to be with her any longer.

Molly deliberately turned her mind to tracking down Adam Humphreys, not an easy task, as it turned out, as he wasn't in the surgeons' lounge or in Theatre, and he wasn't responding to his pager either. She finally traced him to Women's Surgical, where he was checking on a patient he had seen earlier in the evening. He was full of apologies when she politely pointed out that his pager appeared to be switched off. He promised to come straight there and, true to his word, he arrived a couple of minutes later.

Molly knew him quite well and had always found him a pleasant if not very exciting kind of a man. He had asked her out a couple of times, but she had always made an excuse and refused. However, when he repeated his invitation after he had finished examining the X-rays, she found herself accepting. Maybe she should go out with Adam and forget about Sean. Having Sean turn up out of the blue like that had had a highly detrimental effect and she hated the fact that she couldn't seem to get him out of her head. Why, just look at the way she had seriously considered instigating another affair with him! It had been madness, pure, unadulterated madness, to come up with such a crazy plan.

Going out with someone as uncomplicated as Adam Humphreys would help to put her back on track. And who knew what might happen in the future? It could turn out that Adam Humphreys was her Mr Right, the frog who finally turned into her very own prince.

Sean had to bite his tongue when he heard Humphreys asking Molly out on a date. It had nothing to do with him who she dated, he told himself sternly. She was a free agent and he had given up any claim on her two years ago. It was no less than the truth but it was hard to take such a balanced and rational view. For some reason he didn't intend to examine too closely, he couldn't bear the thought of Molly seeing the other man.

The night wore on, the usual mix of the mundane and high drama. Several of the people he saw should have been seen by their GPs rather than turning up at the A&E unit. Sean politely explained that if something of a similar nature occurred again they should contact their local surgery, but he knew that most wouldn't take his advice. Why wait for an appointment when they could be seen immediately? was their view. The fact that it simply added to the pressure the A&E staff were under was of little concern to them.

It was all very depressing and, added to his previous thoughts about Molly and this date she was planning, it had a marked effect. Sean's spirits were at an all-time low when he left the hospital and it didn't help when he saw Molly getting into Adam Humphreys' car. He

knew from what he had overheard her saying that her
car still wasn't fixed and he couldn't blame her for accepting a lift rather than waiting for the bus, but it made
no difference. He didn't want the other man driving her
home, certainly didn't want to think about her inviting
Humphreys in for coffee! Maybe he didn't have any
right to dictate what she did and who she did it with,
but it didn't matter. Deep in his heart, tucked away in
the very darkest corner, lay the truth: he wanted Molly
to belong to him and only him.

Thankfully, Molly managed to get some sleep and
awoke feeling a lot better than she had done. She showered and dressed, taking extra care as she blow-dried
her hair so that it fell in soft red-gold waves around her
face. Adam had asked her if she fancied having lunch
with him that day at one of Dalverston's newest and
most expensive restaurants and she had accepted. It had
seemed propitious to put her plan to forget about Sean
into action as soon as possible.

The restaurant was beautiful if a tad formal for
Molly's taste. She was glad that she had chosen to wear
a smart lilac dress for the lunch date rather than something more casual. The clientele was somewhat older
than her and Adam, although she had to admit that he
seemed very comfortable with the surroundings. He
was obviously well known to the staff too because they
were immediately seated at one of the best tables over-
looking the river. Molly had to hide her amusement as

Adam and the sommelier had a long and intense discussion about the best wine to accompany their lunch. It all seemed slightly over the top to her but she knew that Adam would be very hurt if she let him see how she felt.

Lunches out with Sean had been very different affairs, she found herself thinking as she listened to the two men discussing the merits of Sauvignon Blanc compared to Chablis. One day it had been a picnic of bread and some deliciously crumbly cheese produced by one of the local farms, all washed down with a bottle of beer, while on another occasion they had stopped at a mobile burger bar on the bypass and consumed huge and highly calorific egg and bacon sandwiches. A smile twitched at the corners of her mouth as she remembered how Sean had laughed when the egg had oozed out of her sandwich and dribbled down her chin. Bending forward, he had delicately licked the bright yellow eggy goo away, not something she could imagine Adam doing...

'Excellent! We'll have a bottle of the Chablis, Pierre. I'm sure you will appreciate it, Molly. It has the most exquisite bouquet.'

'I...I'm sure I shall,' Molly replied, hurriedly driving that disturbing thought from her mind as Adam turned to her. She had come here today specifically to stop herself thinking about Sean and she refused to allow her thoughts to get hijacked this early in the date!

She listened attentively as Adam continued with his theme, explaining in great detail the qualities of the various wines. He was obviously something of an expert but Molly could drum up very little enthusiasm for the subject. In her view, wine was wine and you either liked it or you didn't. Spending time discussing it wasn't something she and Sean had ever done—they'd had much better ways to occupy their time!

Once again her thoughts rushed off along their own path and she swallowed her groan of dismay. She didn't want to think about the hours she and Sean had spent lying in each other's arms, certainly didn't want to remember how wonderful it had felt to make love with him. It wasn't fair to Adam to think about another man when he had invited her for this very expensive lunch. No, she wouldn't give Sean Fitzgerald another thought, even if it killed her!

'So which is your very favourite wine, Adam?' she asked, leaning forward and adopting an expression of what she hoped would appear to be deep and undivided interest. Out of the corner of her eye, she saw the head waiter escorting someone to a nearby table. However, it wasn't until the waiter moved away to fetch a menu that Molly realised who it was. All of a sudden her blood began to boil, growing hotter and hotter until it felt as though she would explode. What on earth was Sean doing here?

CHAPTER SEVEN

WHAT IN HEAVEN'S name was he doing here?

Sean could hear the question drumming inside his head as it had been doing for the best part of an hour, yet he still hadn't come up with an answer to it. Or not a truthful one, anyhow. Oh, he had listed at least half a dozen reasons to explain why he'd felt a sudden need to dine in the lap of luxury but he knew in his heart that not one of them was valid. He didn't *really* feel that he deserved a treat after working so hard. Neither did he *honestly* believe it was essential he tried out the restaurant in case he decided to invite someone here for dinner. He had come here today for one reason and one reason only—because Molly would be lunching here with Humphreys. *Hell!*

The waiter returned to take his order and Sean pointed to the first thing on the extensive menu. He had no idea what he'd ordered after the man left and didn't care. He wasn't here for the food. He was here because he couldn't bear the thought of Molly schmoozing with the other man. OK, so he was behaving like the proverbial dog-in-the-manger but so what? Humphreys wasn't right for Molly. Maybe he didn't know much about the other man, granted, but he could tell that just by looking at him. Humphreys was too staid, too solid, too damned reliable—everything *he* wasn't.

Molly needed someone with more pizzazz, someone who would treasure her, appreciate her beauty and her kindness as well as her generosity of spirit. He had appreciated all of those things, even though he had had to let her go. But Humphreys? No way was he right for her and she was making a big mistake if she thought he was!

His lunch arrived and Sean picked up his knife and fork even though the thought of actually eating the food that had been set before him was making his stomach churn. Molly was leaning across the table now, laughing at some comment her companion had made. Sean glowered, hating to hear the sound of her laughter and not be the cause of it. He had enjoyed making her laugh; it had made him feel incredibly happy—happier than he had felt for such a long time. He couldn't bear the thought that some other guy was basking in the same happy glow.

He applied himself to his lunch, wanting to get it over and done with as quickly as possible so he could leave. Coming here had been a huge mistake. Although Molly hadn't acknowledged him in any way, he knew that she had seen him. The thought of having to dredge up one of those pitifully lame excuses if she demanded an explanation for his presence was more than he could handle. To heck with the food; he was leaving this very minute!

Sean pushed back his chair then stopped when he became aware that someone was standing beside his table. He looked up, carefully smoothing his features into a non-committal expression. 'Molly! What a surprise. Are you having lunch here as well?'

'Yes, I am.' She smiled back at him, her green eyes filled with a disturbing mixture of emotions. There was definitely anger there, Sean decided, plus indignation, but as for the rest—well, he couldn't quite work them all out. And before he attempted to do so she rounded on him.

'How dare you, Sean? I've no idea what you think you're doing—'

'Having lunch. Why—what else would I be doing in a place like this?'

'So it's just coincidence that brought you here today?' She gave an unladylike snort of disbelief. 'It hadn't anything to do with the fact that you knew Adam was bringing me here?'

'Of course not. Why should it?'

Sean fixed a smile to his own mouth, desperately trying to play the part of the injured innocent. Admitting that she had hit the nail squarely on its head was out of the question. If he did that then he would have to explain why he had followed her here and that was something he couldn't do. How could he explain this strange compulsion he felt to keep her for himself when he didn't fully understand it himself?

'Someone mentioned that this was *the* place to eat so I thought I would check it out for future reference.'

He gave a small shrug, thinking how beautiful she looked as she stood there glaring down at him. It wasn't often that Molly's temper was roused; she was far too kind and loving to kick up a scene. The only time he had seen her this angry, in fact, was when he had told her that he no longer wanted to see her. He had been far too upset at the time to appreciate the change in her but now he couldn't help noticing how glorious she looked with her green eyes blazing and her wonderful red-gold hair shimmering in a fiery halo around her head. Molly was not only kind, loving and giving—she was a highly passionate woman as well.

'Oh, I see. So what have you decided? Does it meet your requirements or not?'

'Requirements,' Sean echoed, trying to get a grip on his libido, which seemed to think that this was the right moment to make itself known.

'The perfect place to seduce your latest victim, of course.' She glanced around the beautifully appointed dining room and there was both hurt and scorn in her eyes when she turned to him again. 'She must be rather special if you're thinking of shelling out for dinner here. I mean, the prices are a lot steeper than they are at your usual venues but there again you must think she's worth it. Not every woman you go out with is a cheap date, I imagine.'

She spun round on her heel, leaving Sean wondering what he should do. Oh, he knew what she had meant by that last scathing comment—it had been painfully obvious! However, she was wrong—very, very wrong—if she believed he had taken her out to places which hadn't cost the earth because he had thought she wasn't worth anything better. Those picnics and that trip to the burger van had been red-letter occasions for him. Not even the *fanciest* dinners at the *most* upmarket restaurants could compare to them. He had not only enjoyed the food but he'd enjoyed it because of Molly's company and that had raised those occasions to a whole different level. Why, even a meal of bread and water would have tasted like manna from heaven if they had eaten it together!

Sean stood up, determined that he was going to set matters straight. No way was he letting Molly get away with accusing him of such despicable meanness. However, before he could go over to have it out with her, he saw Humphreys return to the table. He gritted his teeth as he watched the other man bend down and whisper something in her ear. Molly laughed as she rose to her feet, smiling up at her companion as he slid his hand under her elbow and led her to the conservatory, where coffee was being served.

Sean felt his insides start to churn. The whole thing smacked of an intimacy that he resented. Bitterly. He wanted nothing more than to follow them and thump

Humphreys on the nose but he knew it was out of the question. Humphreys hadn't done anything wrong. If Molly hadn't wanted him to be so familiar then she would have stopped him. How could *he* follow them and make a scene when it was obviously the last thing Molly wanted?

Sean took a deep breath before he summoned the waiter so he could pay his bill, murmuring something suitably appropriate when the man asked him if he had enjoyed his lunch. Enjoyment wasn't the word he would have used, although Molly probably had a very different opinion. Maybe she hadn't been pleased to see him there but he doubted if it had spoiled the date for her. No, this was just the first of many such occasions for her and Humphreys: exquisite dinners at top-flight restaurants, high-brow concerts, trips to the theatre and the ballet—that was undoubtedly Humphreys' style. Who could blame her if she was seduced by such lavish treatment? The best he'd done was to buy her an egg and bacon roll from a mobile burger van. That really must have impressed her!

Molly wasn't looking forward to seeing Sean that night when she went into work. She was still smarting from what had happened at lunchtime. She simply couldn't believe that he had, quite coincidentally, turned up at that particular restaurant. And yet, on the other hand, what reason did he have for following her there? It wasn't as though he was interested in her, was it? Maybe he *had* been sussing out the place for a future occasion and that thought stung more than all the others. Sean was only doing what he did best—dating a variety of women. So why on earth should it matter to her?

It was a relief when she discovered that he was tied up in Resus as it gave her a breathing space before she had to speak to him. She collected her first patient and took him into the treatment room. Bert Feathers was eighty years old but still very active. He had been taking his dog for a walk when he had slipped on some ice and cut his arm on a broken bottle lying on the footpath. His neighbour had brought him into hospital after he had knocked on her door and asked to borrow a sticking plaster.

'This might sting a bit,' Molly warned him as she cleaned the cut with antiseptic solution. The gash was several inches long, quite deep and needed stitching. She wanted to make sure that it didn't become infected. 'Sorry.'

'Don't you worry, lass. It's fine.' Bert gave her a toothless grin. 'I've had worse than this, believe me.'

'Have you indeed?' Molly picked up a fresh piece of cotton wool with her tweezers and swabbed his arm once more. 'So you're an old hand at being patched up, are you?'

'Aye. I was a hill farmer, you see. We lived too far out of town so we were used to fending for ourselves. Me and my brother, Cedric, were pretty handy with a needle if needs be.' He held out his right arm. 'See that scar? Cut my arm real bad while I was mending the tractor one day. Cedric stitched it up for me and it never gave me a bit of trouble afterwards.'

'He did a good job,' Molly agreed, thinking what a tough life the old man must have led. She could only imagine how painful it must have been to have such a large cut stitched without any form of anaesthetic. 'Do you still have your farm?' she asked as she broke open the seal on a fresh pack of sutures.

'No. I had to give it up after Cedric died. It was too much for me on my own so I sold up and moved into town. I got one of them sheltered housing bungalows in the centre of town. Moving there was the best thing I ever done, as it happens.' Bert nodded at the elderly lady sitting beside him. 'I met Doris there, you see. She lives next door and we're right fond of each other. Never had a lady friend when I was younger—never had time, what with the farm and everything. I've made up for it since, though!'

'Good for you!' Molly laughed in delight. 'You're never too old to fall in love, are you?'

'Definitely not. When the lightning strikes, there's nothing you can do about it.' Bert laughed. 'Me and Doris are getting married next week. We've got the church all booked and we're having a bit of a do after-wards at the Green Man. Thought it was time we put things on a regular footing, you understand. You must come along, Sister. We'd love to have you there to help us celebrate, wouldn't we, Doris? And you too, Doctor.

The more the merrier, as they say, and you'll be very welcome.'

Molly glanced round, suddenly realising that someone had come into the room. Her heart lifted and then just as quickly sank again when she saw Sean. All of a sudden she felt her resolve start to crumble. Although her lunch with Adam had been pleasant enough, it wasn't Adam who had occupied her thoughts for the rest of the day. It made her wonder if she would ever erase Sean from her life. They had spoken for—what?— five minutes, possibly. But she had then spent the next five *hours* thinking about him.

It was as though Sean was imprinted in her consciousness and nothing could remove him, not even spending time with another man...especially not spending time with another man, she corrected herself, remembering how often she had found herself comparing Adam Humphreys to Sean during their lunch date and finding the former decidedly lacking. It had been the same ever since Sean had ended their affair too; she had never met anyone who matched up to him and she wasn't sure if she would. Sean might have broken her heart but he still had a hold over her and it was distressing to admit it. It was an effort to hide how she felt as Sean turned to the elderly couple and smiled.

'I missed the start of the conversation. What are you celebrating?' he asked, leaning his shoulder against the wall.

'I was just telling Sister here that me and Doris are

getting married next week,' Bert explained. 'Friday, at St Marie's church in the town centre. We're having a party afterwards at the Green Man and we'd be delighted if you two young folk came along and helped us celebrate.'

'I'm not sure if it will be possible,' Molly began, hurriedly searching for an excuse to refuse the invitation. Panic swept over her. The last thing she needed was to spend any more time with Sean.

'If you're worried about what shift we're working, there's no need.' Sean turned to her and Molly's heart sank even further when she saw the expression in his eyes. Sean knew exactly what she was thinking and, from the look of it, he had no intention of letting her wriggle out of the invitation. 'I've seen the roster and we're both off next Friday, so we would love to come along. Wouldn't we, Molly?'

Molly had no idea what to say. Short of upsetting Bert and Doris by refusing, there was little she could do except agree. Gritting her teeth, she nodded. Sean grinned at her, obviously enjoying the fact that he had got his own way.

'Great! It will be something to look forward to, won't it, Molly? A lovely lead-up to the Christmas festivities.'

'Yes.' It was difficult to get any words out through her clenched teeth but she would hate him to know how annoyed she felt. 'Did you want me for something?'

'Ah, yes.' There was a note in his voice, a hint of some emotion that made her blood heat as he excused himself and drew her to one side, but Molly refused to speculate on the reason for it. They were discussing a work-related issue, she reminded herself sternly. Anything else was inconsequential. It appeared she'd been right too because there was no trace of anything untoward when he continued.

'The patient in Resus has asked if we can contact his family in India. Apparently, he's a student at the local college and he doesn't have any family living here. There isn't a telephone number where we can reach them so we may need to go through the Embassy. I was hoping that you would be able to sort it out.'

'Of course,' Molly said formally. 'I'll get straight onto the Embassy once I've finished in here.'

'Thanks.' He half turned to leave then paused. 'Did you enjoy your lunch and coffee, by the way? You never gave me the chance to ask what you thought of the restaurant.'

'The food was excellent,' she said shortly, refusing to let him goad her into saying something she would regret. If he'd had an ulterior motive for being there then she didn't want to know what it was. She treated him to a deliberately bright smile. 'Adam and I had a great time, I have to say. In fact, I'm sure we shall go back there again in the future.'

'Good. I'm glad you didn't find it too stuffy.'

He sketched her a wave and headed back to Resus before she could ask him what he meant by that comment. Had Sean found the place rather too formal, as she had done? she wondered as she started suturing Bert's arm. Although the food had been delicious, the restaurant had lacked atmosphere, although maybe that had been down to her companion, she mused. Although Adam was extremely attentive, he lacked any real charisma. Adam certainly wouldn't have been able to make lunching at a burger van feel like a Michelin star experience!

Molly's mouth tightened. Once again she was comparing Adam to Sean and she had to stop. She finished suturing Bert's arm and saw him and Doris out then collected her next patient. She had no intention of wondering who Sean was planning to invite out for an expensive dinner. He could date every single woman in the hospital if he wanted and she wouldn't lose a wink of sleep worrying about it! However, despite such stalwart claims, she couldn't deny that the thought of Sean seeing some other woman hurt. It brought it home to her once more how vital it was that she erased him from her life for good.

CHAPTER EIGHT

SEAN HAD THE next two days off and had decided to spend them looking for a place to live. As it had been a last-minute decision to accept the post in Dalverston he had booked himself into a bed and breakfast, but if he was to spend the next six weeks working here he desperately needed his own space.

He set off early to visit the local estate agent's office and came away with a list of four properties, all available on a short-term lease. However, he quickly discovered that the agency's glowing descriptions fell far short of the reality. By the time he arrived at the last property he was starting to feel very despondent. *Cosy* probably meant tiny and *full of character* undoubtedly meant it was riddled with damp or overrun with mice or both. He almost gave up but the thought of having to put up with living in one room for the next few weeks spurred him on. He would go crazy if he had to stare at the same four walls much longer!

Sean got out of the car. The cottage was tucked away down a narrow lane close to the river and he stood for a moment, drinking in the peace and quiet. He frowned because the area seemed strangely familiar for some reason. Looking around, he realised with a start that it was very close to where Molly lived. Why, he could remember running along this very lane one morning after he had stayed the night at her house! He sighed. It put him in a bit of a quandary. Molly had made it abundantly clear on more than one occasion that she wanted nothing to do with him outside of work, hadn't she? On the other hand, he was pretty much out of options by now, he reasoned, and it wasn't as if he and Molly would be next door neighbours. The thought helped him make up his mind and he went and knocked on the front door. It opened a crack and a wizened face peered out at him.

'Yes?'

'Mrs Bradshaw? I believe you're renting out your cottage. The estate agent gave me the details.' He showed the old lady the letter the agency had given him and smiled at her. 'They said they would ring and let you know I was coming.'

'That's right, dear. Come in, come in.' She opened the door wider and ushered him inside. 'I'm off to New Zealand, you see, to stay with my son and his wife over Christmas. They've asked me umpteen times if I'd go and stay with them but I've always refused in the past because I didn't want to leave Henry.' She sighed. 'He's no longer with us, I'm afraid, so I've no excuse not to go now.'

'I'm so sorry,' Sean said quietly, thinking how sad it

must be to lose one's partner after what must have been a lengthy relationship. 'Were you married a long time?'

'Married?' The old lady laughed. 'Oh, no. Henry wasn't my husband, dear. He died many years ago. Henry was my dog and a bad-tempered old thing too, but I still loved him. He finally went to doggy heaven a month ago so I decided to book my flight. The problem is that I don't like the thought of leaving the cottage standing empty while I'm away. One of my neighbours, who lives just round the corner, did offer to pop in and check everything was all right, but I thought it was too much for her when she's so busy working, which is why I decided to rent it out.'

'I see.' Sean laughed at his mistake then looked around the living room. It was small, admittedly, but it felt wonderfully cosy and inviting. 'This is lovely,' he said truthfully. 'It feels so...well, homely, is the best way to describe it.'

'I'm glad you like it, dear. I've lived here for over forty years and I love the place. Why don't you look round and see if it's suitable for you?' the old lady suggested. 'I'll put the kettle on and make us a cup of tea.'

Sean did as he was told, checking out the small but functional kitchen, the bedroom with its old-fashioned dark wood furniture and the surprisingly large and well-equipped bathroom. He had already decided to take it by the time he returned to the living room and he told Mrs Bradshaw that he would get straight onto the agency.

'That is good news, dear.' Mrs Bradshaw beamed as

she handed him a delicate china cup and saucer. 'I'm so pleased. Not only will I know the place is being well looked after but it means that Molly won't have to bother about it.'

'Molly,' Sean repeated, his hand shaking ever so slightly so that the cup started to rattle in its saucer. He hurriedly set it safely down on the end table, telling himself that he was being silly. It wouldn't be his Molly; that would be too much of a coincidence. No, Mrs Bradshaw's Molly was most likely a kindly older lady like herself. 'Is she a friend of yours?'

'Yes. Molly's a real sweetheart. I'm sure you'll like her. She's been like a daughter to me—pops to the shop for bread and milk if I run out; fetches my Sunday paper if she's not working at the weekend.' Mrs Bradshaw sighed. 'She's a nurse in the A&E department at the hospital and she works the most terrible hours but she still finds the time to visit me. You can understand why I don't want to burden her with having to look after my cottage while I'm away, can't you?'

'I…erm…yes. Of course,' Sean replied, his heart sinking as he realised that he couldn't in all conscience take the cottage now he knew that there was a very real risk of him bumping into Molly.

'Mrs Bradshaw,' he began, knowing that he had no choice in the circumstances other than to tell the old lady that he had changed his mind. Maybe he did love the cottage but it wasn't worth taking it if it meant up-setting Molly.

'It's such a weight off my mind!' the old lady declared, cutting him off mid-flow. She patted his hand. 'Now I shall be able to go off and enjoy my holiday without having to worry. I just know that you will take very good care of everything here, dear.'

'Of course,' Sean murmured because he really couldn't find it in his heart to disappoint her after hearing that.

Maybe there was no need to do so either, he thought as he picked up his cup and drank his tea. He would just have to be extra careful to stay out of Molly's way. After all, with him there, taking care of the cottage, there would be no need for Molly to pop in, would there? By the time he left, he had more or less convinced himself that there was nothing to worry about. After all, he needed somewhere to live and the cottage was perfect for his needs. The downside of living the way he did was that he had never had a real home and all of a sudden he found himself longing for a place of his own.

It was such an unprecedented thought that it threw him completely. Leaving his car parked in the lane, he made his way to the river. It was bitterly cold down there but he didn't notice the chill. Having a home of his own had been all tied up with the plans he and Claire had made for their future together. He had never considered the idea since she had died but there was no point denying how tempting it was and the realisation made him feel overwhelmed with guilt, as though he was betraying Claire by even considering it.

Closing his eyes, he tried to conjure up Claire's image but it just wouldn't come. Her face was hazy, her features too indistinct to see her clearly. Slowly but surely, Claire was slipping away from him and it was painful to know that he was incapable of keeping her safe in his heart where she deserved to be. He had planned to spend his life with her, so what kind of a man must he be if he had allowed her memory to fade?

Unbidden, another image began to form in his mind's eye and Sean felt his breath catch when he recognised the familiar features: those deep green eyes; the long black lashes; that tumble of red-gold curls...

He opened his eyes and stared across the river in despair. He might not be able to recall Claire's face but he had no difficulty at all conjuring up Molly's.

Molly had been planning to go into town to do some much-needed food shopping. However, on a sudden whim, she decided to take the less direct route along by the river. It was a beautiful day, even if it was bitterly cold, and the fresh air would do her good after three days of working nights. She walked to the top of the path and came to a sudden halt when she spotted Sean standing on the riverbank. He was staring across the river and there was an expression of such intense pain on his face that her heart seemed to scrunch up inside her. Even though she knew it wasn't any of her business what was troubling him, she simply couldn't walk on by and leave him like this.

'Hello, Sean,' she said softly as she made her way towards him. He glanced round and she could see the effort it cost him to pull himself together.

'Hello, Molly. What are you doing here? Out for a walk?'

'Hmm. I needed to get some shopping so I thought I'd kill two birds with one stone and get some fresh air at the same time.' She pushed her hands deep into her pockets, afraid that she would do something really stupid like touching him. Maybe he *was* hurting but there was no reason to think that he would welcome her concern.

'So what brings you here?' she asked brightly, not wanting to dwell on that thought. 'Are you out for a walk as well?'

'No, actually, I was viewing a house that I'm hoping to rent.' He turned and pointed back up the path. 'It's just up there, Lilac Cottage—the last cottage in the row.'

'You don't mean Mrs Bradshaw's cottage!' she exclaimed and he grimaced.

'Yes. I had a feeling that you wouldn't be too pleased if you found out I was living so close to you. Not to worry. I shall tell the letting agents that I've changed my mind.' He turned to walk back up the path but Molly shook her head.

'There's no reason why you should do that. I really don't care where you live, Sean. Plus I know for a fact that Mrs Bradshaw has been very worried about finding someone suitable to rent the cottage while she's away.'

She gave a careless little shrug, determined not to let him know how disturbing she found the idea of him living so close to her. It wasn't only in work that she would have to take steps to avoid him, it seemed. 'If you think the cottage is right for you then you should take it.'

'Are you sure?' he asked and her skin prickled when she heard the doubt in his voice. It was obvious that he didn't think she could cope with them living in such close proximity and she needed to squash that idea right away.

'Of course I'm sure! It's you who's making such a big deal of it, not me.' Molly deliberately shifted the conversation along a different path, not wanting to have to keep on reassuring him when, in truth, she felt so ambivalent about the idea. 'Why are you so eager to move in the first place? I wouldn't have thought it was worth it when you're only going to be in Dalverston for such a short time.'

'You're right, and normally I wouldn't dream of swapping and changing. However, it was a last-minute decision to accept this job and the only accommodation I could find was a room in a B&B close to the bypass.' He shrugged. 'It's all right but I'm starting to get cabin fever from staring at the same four walls all the time. At least I'll have a bit more space in the cottage.'

'It must be odd to keep moving around all the time,' Molly observed thoughtfully. 'Have you never wanted a place of your own?'

'No. Well, not until recently, anyway.' His voice was

low but laced with so much anguish that it immediately made her set aside any qualms she had. Reaching out, she touched his hand.

'Why, what's happened to make you change your mind recently?'

'I'm not sure. Maybe it's being here—who knows?' He turned his hand over and captured hers. 'I don't want to feel this way, believe me, but I can't seem to stop. And it makes me feel so damned guilty!'

'Guilty? I don't understand. Why should you feel guilty about wanting a home of your own?' It was impossible to keep the surprise out of her voice and she heard him sigh.

'It doesn't matter. Take no notice of me. It's probably a case of the midwinter blues.' He gave her a tight smile as he let go of her hand and started to walk back up the path, but if he thought he could fob her off like that he could think again.

'Of course it matters!' Molly declared fiercely. She stepped directly in his path so that he was forced to stop. 'It's obvious that something's troubling you, Sean, so what is it? Surely it can't be whether or not to buy yourself a house. I mean, that would be crazy!'

'Maybe it seems crazy to you, but the situation is far more complicated than it appears.'

He gently eased her aside but there was such pain on his face that Molly knew she couldn't let him leave. Catching hold of his arm, she held him fast. Maybe it didn't have anything to do with her but Sean was hurting and she wanted to help him any way she could.

'Then tell me about it.' She stared into his eyes, willing him to trust her, wondering if he would. 'I know things haven't been exactly easy between us, Sean, but I want to help you. Really I do.'

Sean leant forward in the chair, warming his hands in the heat coming from the fire. He felt cold to the core, as though his very flesh and bones had turned to ice. The rational part of his brain knew that he'd been mad to let Molly persuade him to come home with her but the other part didn't care. He couldn't bear it if he had to spend the rest of his days eaten up by guilt for the part he had played in Claire's death. For ten long years he had kept it to himself; even his family didn't know the full story. But maybe it was time that he brought it all out into the open and faced the criticism that would undoubtedly follow. It had to be better than living like this—knowing he was to blame and constantly trying to avoid thinking about it.

'Here we go. Hot chocolate to warm us up. I don't know about you but I'm absolutely frozen!'

Molly came back with a tray bearing two steaming mugs of chocolate. Sean nodded his thanks as she placed one of the mugs on the table next to his chair. Going over to the sofa, she sat down, curling her legs under her, and the very normality of the scene helped to ease a little of the tension that gripped him. Reaching for his own mug, he cradled it between his hands, relishing the heat that flowed through his icy finger-tips. He had no idea what Molly would think once he told her the whole sorry tale; he would just have to deal with it whichever way he could.

'So, are you going to tell me what's wrong?'

Her voice was gentle. Sean knew that if he changed his mind she wouldn't push him. It was up to him if he confessed what he had done—how his actions had re-sulted in the death of the woman he had been planning to marry. Just for a moment, he wavered, unsure if he could face the condemnation that would surely follow. However, the thought of continually feeling this way was more than he could bear. Even facing Molly's re-vulsion couldn't be any worse than this.

'It's all to do with Claire and what happened to her.' He placed the mug on the table when he felt his hands start to tremble. The only way he would get through this was by keeping a tight rein on his emotions. Once he lost control of them then all the remorse and guilt that had consumed him these past years would come spilling out and he couldn't bear to think that Molly would witness it.

'Who was she? Your girlfriend, I assume.' Molly's voice was just as gentle and undemanding and Sean felt a little more tension seep out of him.

'Yes. Well, she was my fiancée, actually. We were childhood sweethearts; I suppose that's how people would describe us. Our parents were friends so we grew up together. We were both only children, you see, and it was great to have a sort of surrogate sister to play with.'

'I see. I can understand how close you must have been,' she said softly.

'We were, very close, right through school and on into university. Claire studied law at Liverpool while I went to Cambridge and did medicine so we didn't see much of one another, but it didn't make any difference. We just picked up where we'd left off whenever we met up.' He shrugged. 'It seemed only natural that we should get engaged once we had qualified. Both our families were thrilled, as you might expect, and set about planning our wedding.'

He tailed off, not sure how to tell her the rest. What would Molly think once he told her the truth? Would she blame him, as he blamed himself? Even though it shouldn't have mattered what she thought, he knew deep in his heart that it did.

'We were both working incredibly hard, trying to establish our careers,' he continued before his courage deserted him. 'Claire had been accepted for pupillage at a leading firm of barristers in London and I was working as a junior registrar at a London hospital in A&E. Although we shared a flat, we actually saw very little of one another.'

'It's difficult to find time for a relationship when you're starting out on your career,' Molly agreed, and he sighed.

'That's what I told myself, especially when we fell

out, as we seemed to do with increasing frequency. I told myself that we just needed to get through the next few months and it would get easier once we were married, but the situation grew worse, if anything. It got so bad that I avoided going home some nights, just to get a break from all the arguing. And then one night Claire phoned me at work and told me that she needed to speak to me urgently. I wasn't off duty until eight p.m. so I arranged to meet her at a bar we sometimes went to.

'It was one of those nights you learn to dread, as it turned out. Dozens of patients, all with major complications. There was no chance of my being able to leave on time so I phoned Claire and explained that I couldn't make it. She was already there, waiting for me, and I could tell she was upset when I cancelled, but there was nothing I could do about it.'

He broke off, steeling himself to tell Molly the rest of the story. He had reached the real crux of his tale, the part that he found it the most difficult to voice. He took a steadying breath before he continued in a voice that was devoid of any emotion.

'That was the last time I ever spoke to her. She left the bar a short time later and was hit by a taxi while she was crossing the road. She died instantly. One of the bar staff said at the inquest that she had been crying when she had left—and that was all down to me, Molly. If I hadn't been so curt with her then she would never have stepped in front of that cab.'

CHAPTER NINE

MOLLY HAD NO idea what to say. She was so stunned by what Sean had told her that her thoughts were in a complete turmoil. And then, slowly, one thought rose through all the confusion in her head: Sean wasn't to blame. It had been an accident, a tragic and terrible accident.

'It wasn't your fault!' She got up from the sofa and went to kneel beside his chair. 'It was an accident, Sean, awful, I know, but you can't blame yourself for what happened.'

'No? So why does it feel like it's my fault?' He shook his head. 'No, if I hadn't been so offhand with her then Claire would never have got so upset. She'd told me that she needed to speak to me urgently and I should have realised that it had to be something really important.'

'Do you have any idea what she wanted to tell you?' Molly asked hesitantly then immediately wished that she hadn't when she saw how tormented he looked.

'Oh, yes. It came out at the inquest.' He took a deep breath but she could hear the torment in his voice.

'Claire was pregnant when she was killed—roughly eight weeks, according to the coroner. I had no idea but it makes no difference, does it? I'm not only responsible for Claire's death but for the death of our baby as well.'

Molly couldn't think of anything to say. The sheer horror of what he must have been through was simply too much to take in. And it was obvious that Sean had misinterpreted her silence. He laughed harshly as he stood up.

'I can tell by your expression what you think, Molly, and I don't blame you. I mean, what kind of a man doesn't even suspect his fiancée is pregnant, especially when she's sending out all the right signals?'

'Wh...what sort of signals?' she murmured, getting to her feet as well.

'All the rows, of course. Claire was never the sort of person to start an argument—she was far too quiet. I should have realised that something was going on and made her tell me what it was, but I was too preoccupied with my job and with making a good impression.'

'But that's ridiculous! You had no way of knowing that she was pregnant unless she chose to tell you. I mean, why did she wait so long? Surely it would have been far more in character for her to tell you the moment she suspected that she might be having a baby?'

'She probably would have done if I hadn't been so completely wrapped up in my work.' He gave her a grim smile. 'I was far too busy to find the time to sit down and talk to her.'

'She must have been busy too,' Molly pointed out. 'You said that you were both trying to make a go of your careers.'

'Yes. But it doesn't negate what I did or, rather, what I didn't do. I wasn't there when Claire needed me and because of that she and the baby died.' His voice broke. 'And I will have to live with that every day of my life.'

Molly acted instinctively then. Perhaps if she had been thinking clearly she wouldn't have done what she did but every instinct she possessed was urging her to comfort him. Reaching out, she drew him into her arms and held him, simply held him, hoping that he might take comfort from the closeness of another human being. She had never suspected that Sean—live-for-the-moment Sean—was carrying such a burden around with him, but somehow she had to make him understand that he wasn't to blame for what had happened.

If she could.

The thought that he might live out the rest of his days blaming himself for the tragedy brought a rush of tears to her eyes. Molly tried to hold them back but more kept on coming, pouring down her face in a relentless torrent. She realised all of a sudden that she wasn't crying only for him but for herself as well. Sean must have loved Claire so very much, far more than he could ever have loved her, and it was almost too painful to bear to know that she could never have matched the other woman in his affections.

'Molly?' She felt him go still before he slowly set

her away from him. Bending, he looked into her face. 'You're crying.'

'Take no notice.' She sniffed loudly, hunting in her pocket for a tissue and typically not finding one. She couldn't bear it if he guessed just how devastated she felt, couldn't add to his burden in any way. It wasn't Sean's fault that his heart belonged to another woman.

'Here.' Sean plucked a tissue from the box on the coffee table but, instead of handing it to her, he tipped up her face and gently wiped away her tears. Tossing the soggy tissue into the waste bin, he smiled at her. 'Better now?'

'Yes. Thank you.' She went to move away but his hands fastened lightly around the top of her arms and held her fast.

'I'm sorry, Molly. I never meant to upset you like this.'

'I know. It's just that I can't bear to think of you blaming yourself when there's no need,' she said, deliberately blanking out any thoughts about how she felt. It was Sean who needed consoling, not her.

'Isn't there?' He sighed as he drew her into his arms and held her against him. 'I wish I could believe that.'

'Then you must try harder,' she said fiercely. She pulled back and glared at him, determined to make him see sense. 'It was an accident, Sean. A tragic accident, but you weren't to blame!'

'Oh, Molly, I want to believe you. Really I do.'

He drew her to him once more, planting a gentle kiss

on her cheek. It was meant to be no more than a token, a simple expression of gratitude for her support, and it might have remained that way too if she hadn't chosen that precise moment to turn her head. Molly froze when she felt his lips glide from her cheek and come to rest at the corner of her mouth. She knew that she should do something to stop what was happening, but it was as though her body was suddenly refusing to obey her. When his lips started to move again, but deliberately this time, she could only stand there, motionless.

His mouth found hers and she heard him sigh, felt the warm expulsion of his breath on her lips, and it was that which broke the spell. However, if she'd hoped that it would bring her to her senses she was mistaken. Her lips seemed to possess a will of their own as they clung to his, eagerly inviting him to continue. And he did.

Molly moaned when she felt the tip of his tongue start to explore the contours of her mouth. She could taste the richness of the chocolate he had drunk on his tongue and it merely heightened her desire for him. Opening her mouth, she allowed him all the licence he needed to deepen the kiss and he wasn't slow to take advantage. They were both breathing heavily when they broke apart, both shaken by the speed and the depth of their need for one another. They might not have planned on kissing but Molly knew that neither of them could deny that it had had a profound effect on them both.

'I didn't mean for this to happen, Molly.'

'I know.' She gave a little shrug then stilled when she

felt desire scud through her once more as his hands slid from her shoulders and down her arms. It had always been this way, she thought sadly. Sean had only needed to touch her and her blood had raced. And the most terrifying realisation of all was that nothing had changed.

'I never planned it either,' she said huskily, trying to damp down the fear that engulfed her. She didn't want to feel how she had felt two years ago, definitely didn't want to risk having her heart broken once more. Now, more than ever, she needed to be sensible—now that she knew about Claire. She had to nip these feelings in the bud before they could grow into something even bigger and far more dangerous.

'I suppose we should put it down to the heat of the moment. Everything got a bit tense just now, didn't it?' His hands skimmed back up her arms and came to rest against her collarbone. Molly could feel the coolness of his fingers seeping into her heated flesh through the thickness of her woollen sweater and shivered.

'It did.' She dredged up a smile. 'My crying like that probably didn't help either. Sorry.'

'Don't apologise. I was touched that you felt that way.' He returned her smile. 'You always did have a tender heart, Molly.'

'In other words, I was a soft touch,' she retorted, deliberately whipping up her anger in the hope that it would help set her back on track. 'It's a good job I've decided to make some changes to how I behave. There will be no more wearing my heart on my sleeve in future, believe me!'

'So today was a one-off, was it? You'll be hard-hearted Molly from now on?'

'Yes!' Molly declared roundly when she heard the teasing note in his voice and realised that he didn't believe her. The last thing she wanted was for Sean to think she was a pushover. 'I'm going to concentrate on what *I* want for a change.'

'Then I'm glad that we had this conversation today.' He brushed his knuckles down her cheek. 'I feel a lot better than I did, Molly, and it's all thanks to you.'

'I'm glad,' she said huskily, so touched by the admission that her anger immediately melted away. 'So does that mean you'll think about what I said, about you not being to blame? It was an accident, Sean, and it wasn't your fault.'

'I'll try.'

Although he agreed readily enough, Molly had a feeling that it would never actually happen. Sean was determined to blame himself for the tragedy and it hurt to know that his life would be blighted for ever by it. Reaching up, she cupped his face between her hands.

'Then you must try really hard!' Her voice caught. 'I can't bear to think of you ruining your life this way.'

'Oh, Molly!'

Turning, he pressed his mouth against her palm and she shuddered when she felt desire spike through her once more. When she felt the tip of his tongue start to stroke her skin, she moaned softly. It was almost too much to feel the light moist pressure of his tongue caressing her flesh. Closing her eyes, she gave herself up to the moment, blanking out any thoughts about the wisdom of what she was doing. She didn't want to think—she just wanted to feel.

The tip of his tongue moved from her palm to her wrist, lavishing it with the same attention. Molly had never realised before that her wrist could be an erogenous zone and closed her eyes, savouring the moment. Kisses were fine but this was different. This gentle act of seduction implied an intimacy that she had never expected. Maybe she was mistaken but she couldn't imagine that Sean had done this with many women.

The thought filled her with a sudden sense of peace. One of the hardest things to deal with had been the thought that she had been just one of many women in Sean's life. However, the gentle pressure of his tongue as it moved over the delicate inner skin of her wrist put paid to that; it made her feel special. Wanted. Cherished.

He raised his head and his eyes were so dark that they appeared almost black as he looked at her. 'I know I shouldn't be doing this but I can't help myself,' he said hoarsely. 'Tell me to stop, Molly, if it isn't what you want.'

Molly bit her lip, unsure of what she wanted. Oh, she didn't want him to stop—that was a given. But was it wise to let this go any further, to risk falling under his spell all over again? He had hurt her so badly and she didn't think that she could go back to that dark place again. But if she called a halt then would she regret it, always wish that she had taken the risk in the hope that it might bring her closure?

'I don't know what I want, Sean. Part of me is terrified at the thought of feeling like I did two years ago. I can't go back there. I don't think I could bear it.'

'Oh, sweetheart, don't! Please don't upset yourself because I behaved like such a crass idiot.' He tipped up her chin and kissed her lightly on the mouth. 'I regret it more than I can ever tell you, Molly.'

'Do you?' she whispered, her blood humming inside her veins at the feel of his lips on hers.

'Yes. I hurt you and I never meant to do that. It's just that I found it so hard to do what was right.' He brushed her mouth with another sensual kiss. 'I knew I should end our relationship but I kept putting it off, and there's no excuse for that.'

'Why did you keep putting it off?' she asked, her breath coming in rapid little spurts so that it sounded as though she was having difficulty breathing, which she was. Being held in Sean's arms like this, having him kiss her, was making her feel breathless... *As well as a lot of other things.*

Sean knew that he shouldn't answer that question. Admitting that he had delayed ending their relationship because he couldn't bear to part with her wouldn't help either of them. It was all in the past and it should remain in the past too. And yet some tiny part of his brain was insisting that he told Molly the truth, that he should hold up his hands and confess why he'd had such problems letting her go. Surely he owed her that much at the very least?

'Because I hated the thought of being without you.' He rested his forehead against hers, not wanting to look into her eyes in case he weakened. 'That time we spent together was one of the happiest times of my life and I wanted it to continue, even though I knew it couldn't.'

'Because of Claire?'

He heard the catch in her voice and hated to think that he might be causing her yet more pain. But it was two years since they'd parted: she'd had two years to get over him. The thought helped to steady him even if it didn't come as the relief it should have been.

'Yes. I made a vow after Claire died that I would remain true to her memory and I can't break it, Molly, not for any reason or anyone.'

'I understand, Sean. Really I do.'

She stepped back, deliberately setting some distance between them, and Sean had to stop himself hauling her back into his arms and telling her that he had changed his mind. He felt bereft without her in his arms, empty, incomplete. It took every atom of willpower he could muster not to say too much but he mustn't mislead her. After the heat of the moment had passed then he would regret breaking his vow...

Wouldn't he?

'Thank you.' His voice grated and he cleared his

throat, unable to deal with all the conflicting emotions rioting around inside him. Did he really want to let Claire go and look to the future? Could he bear to do so when he might be consumed by guilt for ever? He had to be sure because he couldn't play with Molly's emotions, couldn't lead her to believe that they had a future together when in all likelihood it wouldn't amount to anything.

'There's nothing to thank me for.' She gave a little shrug and he almost weakened when he realised how brave she was being. However, it would be wrong to allow this to go any further, so very wrong to risk hurting her all over again.

Sean's heart was heavy as he said goodbye and made his way to the door. Molly saw him out although she didn't wait to wave him off, not that he could blame her. She was probably glad to see the back of him after what he had told her. He stood in the road for a moment, sucking in great gulps of the frosty air. It should have been a relief to tell her about Claire and explain his reasons for breaking up with her but it wasn't relief he felt. Not right now anyway. Maybe relief would come later but at the moment all he felt was a deep sense of sadness for what he could have had if things had been different.

If he hadn't made that vow then he could have had Molly in his life. For ever and always.

CHAPTER TEN

SURPRISINGLY, SEAN DISCOVERED that he did feel better after his talk with Molly. He wasn't sure why when it had thrown up so many other issues but it felt as though some of the weight had been lifted off his shoulders. There was a definite spring to his step when he went into work two days later but, sadly, it didn't last very long. One glimpse of Molly chatting to Adam Humphreys soon put paid to it. Even though he knew it was wrong, he hated to see her with another man.

Fortunately, the department was as busy as ever so he had no time to brood. There'd been a car crash on the bypass which resulted in several casualties being brought in at more or less the same time. Molly was doing triage that day and she quickly dispensed with the less seriously injured, leaving him to deal with the rest. However, it was only when the paramedics rushed the trolley into Resus that Sean discovered one of the casualties was Joyce Summers, the most senior Sister on the unit.

'Let's get her on the bed.' Sean did the count as they

quickly moved Joyce off the trolley. She was receiving oxygen as her Sats were worryingly low. She was unconscious and had been since the paramedics had arrived at the scene. She had suffered a serious head injury and Sean's heart sank as he ordered a CT scan because he knew it would be touch and go whether she pulled through. Molly had followed the ambulance crew into Resus and she asked if she could accompany Joyce to Radiography.

'Of course,' Sean agreed immediately. He sighed as he watched her help the porters wheel the bed out of Resus. If Joyce didn't make it then he knew that Molly would be terribly upset and he hated to think of her suffering that way.

He forced his mind back to the job as he set about dealing with the second casualty, a young man called Sam Prentice who, thankfully, wasn't as seriously injured. He had several broken ribs which were causing him some problems breathing. Sean suspected—rightly so—that Sam had a haemothorax and set about sorting it out with the help of Steph Collins, their F1 student. It was the first time that Steph had performed the procedure so Sean guided her through it, showing her how to insert the needle through the tough intercostal muscles between the patient's ribs while they drew off the blood that had collected in the pleural cavity and was compromising Sam's breathing. By the time they had done that, Joyce was back so Sean left Steph to keep an eye on their patient while he went to check the results of the CT scan. It was immediately apparent that it wasn't good news.

'Heavy bleeding on the left side of the brain,' Sean observed, pointing to the area in question. 'The blow to the right side of her head must have carried enough force to knock the brain sideways and cause it to collide with her skull. She's going to need immediate surgery.'

'What are her chances?' Molly asked and his heart ached when he heard the catch in her voice.

'Not good, I'm afraid.' He sighed. 'The bleed is extensive and even if the surgeon manages to stop it then there's probably going to be extensive brain damage.'

'It's so unfair. Joyce is due to retire this Christmas and she and her husband have a whole list of things they are planning to do, including her dream holiday, cruising around the Caribbean.'

'You're right. It isn't fair,' Sean said quietly. He dredged up a smile, wishing there was more he could say by way of comfort. However, he understood better than most how one's plans could alter in mere seconds. 'All we can do is hope that things aren't as bad as they appear.'

Molly didn't say anything. Sean suspected that she didn't believe it any more than he did. He went to the phone and asked for one of the neurosurgical team to attend, aware that his efforts to reassure Molly had failed dismally. He sighed. There was very little else he could have said as it wouldn't have been fair to raise her hopes but it didn't stop him feeling bad about it.

He frowned as that thought sank into his consciousness. If only he had thought harder about being fair
when they had been seeing one another then maybe he
wouldn't have ended up making such a hash of things.
He had known for weeks that he should end their affair
but he had kept putting it off because he hadn't wanted
to let her go. He had behaved with the utmost selfish-
ness and he would always regret it.

Molly deserved someone better than him, someone
without all his attendant baggage. Someone like Adam
Humphreys, for instance—steady, reliable, ready and
eager to make a commitment. Quite frankly, he should
be glad that she had met someone like Humphreys but
as he went back to his patient Sean knew that it wasn't
happiness he felt, not by a long chalk. Right or wrong,
but he couldn't bear the thought of Molly falling in love
with the other man.

Sean tried to put that thought out of his mind but,
typically, it seemed that Humphreys was never out of
the department. Every time he turned round, he spotted Molly and Humphreys chatting to one another. Fair
enough, most of their conversation was related to their
patients but Sean could feel his irritation rising each
time he came across them. Surely the guy could tell that
he needed to give Molly some breathing space rather
than…than bombard her this way! He did his best to
ignore them but when he happened to overhear Humphreys inviting her out for dinner that coming Friday,
he finally flipped. No way was Molly spending the eve-

ning with Humphreys. Not while there was any breath left in his body!

'I hate to butt in, guys, but you already have plans for Friday, Molly.' He smiled as Molly turned to him in surprise. 'It's Bert and Doris's wedding reception— remember?'

'I'm sure they aren't really expecting us to go,' Molly said shortly, glaring at him. 'They probably only asked us for politeness' sake.'

'Not at all.' Sean held his smile although the way Molly was glowering at him would have made a less determined man waver. 'In fact, Bert assured me that they're both looking forward to seeing us there.'

It was only the smallest distortion of the truth but Sean crossed his fingers anyway. Bert had said that he and Doris would be delighted to see them when he had issued the invitation but he had no intention of explaining that to Molly.

'When did you speak to him?' Molly demanded.

'Oh, I'm not sure—a few days ago,' Sean replied, crossing the fingers on his other hand as well. 'It doesn't really matter, does it? I mean I'd hate to disappoint them, wouldn't you?' He turned to Humphreys and grimaced. 'Sorry to scupper your plans, and all that. But it's important to keep a promise, don't you agree?'

'I…erm… Yes, of course.' Adam Humphreys both looked and sounded decidedly put out but Sean didn't care.

Sean turned to Molly, smiling winningly at her.

'We'll sort out the time nearer to the day. At least I won't have to drive very far to pick you up.' He laughed. 'I'm moving into the cottage this week so we'll be living just around the corner from each other very soon.'

He didn't say anything else as he went to fetch his next patient; however, he could tell that Molly was seething about the way he had railroaded her into falling in with his plans. Tough luck, he thought, as he headed to Reception. Although Humphreys might appear perfect on paper, he wasn't right for Molly. He was convinced about that—

'What the hell do you think you're doing?'

Sean stopped dead when Molly came hurrying after him. That she was furiously angry was obvious and he experienced a momentary qualm. Maybe he shouldn't have interfered like that but the thought of her and Humphreys getting cosy was more than he could swallow. He adopted an expression of bewilderment as he turned to face her.

'I'm sorry…?'

'Don't give me that!' She put her hands on her hips and glared at him. 'You know exactly what you've done. You, quite deliberately too, came up with that to stop me going out with Adam, didn't you?'

'I merely reminded you that you had a previous engagement,' Sean replied in his most ingenuous tone. He shrugged. 'I'm sure you don't want to disappoint Bert and Doris, do you?'

'No. But that's not the point, is it?'

'Isn't it? So why do you imagine I butted in to your conversation like that?' he said evenly although his heart was thumping. Did he really want Molly to guess just how much he hated the thought of her dating Humphreys when it would give rise to so many awkward questions?

'I have no idea,' she began and then stopped abruptly when a middle-aged man came hurrying in through the main doors. 'Oh, that's Joyce's husband—Ted. He's going to be devastated when he finds out what's happened to her.'

'Take him into the relatives' room and we'll talk to him in there,' Sean said quickly, hating himself for feeling so relieved at the interruption. 'Once we've explained what's happened then maybe you can take him up to Recovery. Joyce should be finished in Theatre soon and I'm sure he will want to see her.'

'What if she didn't make it?' Molly said with a catch in her voice.

'Then we would have heard by now.' He reached over and squeezed her hand. 'I left a message with the theatre sister to phone us if anything happened.'

'Oh, right. Well, I suppose that's a good sign,' she said quietly.

Sean let her go, watching as she hurried over to Joyce's husband and led him towards the relatives' room. He went to the phone and called Recovery to get an update on Joyce's condition. She had come through the operation successfully but she was being kept sedated as it was hoped that it would help her brain to heal. Although the person he spoke to didn't say as much, he knew that it was still touch and go. Now he had to try and explain all of that to Joyce's husband the least stressful way he could.

Molly sat quietly as she listened to Sean explaining the extent of Joyce's injuries to Ted Summers. He didn't try to paint a brighter picture but carefully and methodically outlined the difficulties Joyce faced. Molly's heart ached when she heard the compassion in his voice. Sean had always been marvellous with grieving relatives and now she understood why he was able to empathise with them to such an extent. He had been on the receiving end of devastating news like this when Claire had died and he had first-hand knowledge of how it felt to have your hopes and dreams ripped apart.

It made her anger over the way he had butted into her conversation with Adam seem very trivial. Maybe she didn't understand his reasons for doing so but it obviously wasn't jealousy at the thought of her and Adam going out together, not when she could hear the underlying grief in his voice. Sean was remembering Claire, recalling how devastated he had felt when he had lost her; how devastated he still felt, in fact. Molly found herself suddenly wishing with every fibre of her being that one day he would be able to move on, even if she wouldn't be around to help him.

'I'm sorry the news isn't better, Ted. All I can say is that Joyce has come this far and that's a positive sign.'

Sean stood up, bringing an end to the meeting. 'I'm sure you must want to see her so Molly is going to take you to Recovery. Joyce will be moved from there to ICU very shortly.'

'Thank you.' Ted Summers rose shakily to his feet. He looked completely poleaxed by what he had heard and Molly hurriedly got up and put a guiding hand under his elbow to lead him to the door.

'There's no need to rush back, Molly. It's not that busy in here so take as long as you need.'

'Right. Thank you.' Molly glanced back, feeling her heart scrunch up inside her. It was only Sean who could make the decision to put the past behind him; no one else could make it for him. And the thought that he might never get over losing Claire was so painful that it was hard to hide how much it upset her.

'Are you all right?' he said softly and she knew that he had noticed she was upset but had assumed it was because of Joyce.

'Yes. I'm fine.'

She turned away, not wanting to burden him with her feelings. Sean had enough to contend with and it would be wrong to encumber him with anything else. She had to deal with her own emotions and come to terms with the situation as it was. The sooner she did that too, the better.

The rest of the week passed and Friday rolled around. Molly had seen very little of Sean, as it happened. He had agreed to swap shifts with his opposite number, who needed time off that coming weekend to visit an ailing relative. While she was glad of the respite, she had to admit that she missed him. Sean was fun to have around, always bright and cheerful and ready to lend a hand. In fact, the department didn't seem the same without him, although maybe it was a good thing that he wasn't there if it gave her a chance to get used to being without him. She must never forget that Sean's time in Dalverston was strictly limited.

By the time she left work on Friday evening, Sean still hadn't contacted her to arrange when he would pick her up to attend Bert and Doris's wedding reception. Molly made her way home, assuring herself that she was relieved that he had apparently changed his mind. An evening watching the box was far preferable to one spent agonising over matters she couldn't change.

She changed into a comfy old tracksuit and settled down in front of the television with her supper on a tray. When the doorbell rang she was engrossed in the latest episode of her favourite soap opera and reluctantly got up to answer it. She'd had several visits from local children out carol singing so she fetched her purse before opening the door then gasped in surprise when she found Sean standing on her step.

'What are you doing here?'

'Collecting you so we can go to Bert and Doris's do.' He frowned as he took stock of what she was wearing. 'I'm sorry. Am I too early?'

'Seeing as we never agreed on a time, then no, you aren't,' Molly replied testily, overwhelmingly aware of how awful she looked in the ratty old tracksuit.

'Oh, no! I never phoned you, did I?' He slapped his forehead with the palm of his hand. 'I've been so busy moving my stuff into the cottage that it went straight out of my mind. Sorry!'

'It's OK.' Molly shrugged, not wanting it to appear as though it mattered an iota. Nevertheless, the thought that she was so easily forgettable didn't exactly cheer her up. She pushed that foolish thought aside. 'As you can see, I'm not ready so it's probably best if you go without me...'

'Not at all,' Sean said quickly. 'There's plenty of time for you to get changed.' He held up his hand when she started to speak. 'I know for a fact that Bert and Doris will be very disappointed if you don't go tonight, Molly.' His voice dropped, sounding so deep and seductive that a shiver ran through her. 'Me too. I've been looking forward to this evening all week.'

Molly knew that she should stand firm but the note of longing in his voice was her undoing. Stepping back, she ushered him into the sitting room, telling herself that it was ridiculous to imagine that Sean was so desperate for her company. It was probably one of his many ruses, she told herself as she hurried upstairs. A trick he had used umpteen times before to get his own way. However, despite all that, she simply couldn't find it in her heart to refuse to go with him and she sighed as she went into the bathroom and turned on the shower. Where Sean was concerned, she was like putty in his hands—pliable, malleable and far too easily led astray!

CHAPTER ELEVEN

THE GREEN MAN was crowded when they arrived. It appeared that Bert and Doris had invited every single person they knew to help them celebrate their marriage. Sean grabbed hold of Molly's hand as they made their way through the fray to where their hosts were seated, not wanting them to become separated. It had been pure good luck that he had managed to persuade her to come tonight after that mistake he had made and he didn't intend to waste a single precious second of her company.

He glanced at her, feeling his heart lift as once again he found himself thinking how lovely she looked. She had chosen a slim-fitting deep green dress for the occasion. If he'd been better versed in fashion-speak he would have been able to describe it in detail but all he knew was that the soft velvety fabric clung to every delectable curve. She was wearing high-heeled shoes and her legs looked fabulous—long and shapely—as she led the way through a gap in the crowd.

Sean swallowed a sigh as he forced his gaze away from the enticing curve of her calves. She looked gorgeous and, what was more, she *was* gorgeous inside and out. No wonder he was having the devil of a job behaving sensibly. One of the reasons why he had agreed to swap shifts was the fact that it would give him a breathing space. Taking some time out away from Molly had seemed propitious and it had worked too. Or it had done until she had opened the door tonight and he had found himself right back where he had started; right back where he had left off two years ago, if he was honest. It couldn't carry on this way—he couldn't cope! At some point he would have to make some decisions about what he intended to do, but not tonight. Tonight he was just going to enjoy being with her.

'So you made it. That's grand, that is. We did wonder if you'd come as we know how busy you both must be, what with your work and everything.' Bert Feathers beamed in delight as he stood up to greet them and Sean hastily returned his thoughts to the reason why they were there. Bending, he kissed Doris's cheek.

'We've been really looking forward to tonight, haven't we, Molly?' Sean said as he straightened up.

'I...um... Yes, of course.' Molly bent and kissed Doris then gave Bert a kiss as well. 'Congratulations to you both. I'm sure you'll be very happy together.'

'Oh, there's no doubt about that!' Bert laughed as he sat down and squeezed Doris's hand. 'We plan to make the most of whatever time we have left, don't we, love, starting tomorrow with our honeymoon.'

'Where are you going?' Sean asked, trying to hide

his chagrin at the way Molly had hesitated. He knew that he had railroaded her into coming with him so it shouldn't have been a surprise if she appeared less than thrilled about spending the evening with him; however, the thought that she would have preferred Humphreys' company to his didn't sit easily with him.

'The Canary Islands. We're flying to Tenerife in the morning and spending Christmas and New Year there,' Bert informed them happily. 'I've never been on a plane before, never even had a holiday, in fact, unless you count a day trip to Scarborough when I was a lad, so this will be a first for me. I'm right looking forward to it, too. So's Doris.'

'How wonderful!' Sean exclaimed, genuinely delighted for them. Another couple of guests came over to speak to them at that moment so he and Molly moved aside. People were milling about, chatting to friends or sampling the buffet which had been arranged on long trestle tables at the far side of the room. Sean grimaced when his stomach rolled at the thought of the delicious-looking spread and he saw Molly look at him.

'I never got chance to eat anything today. I was too busy putting things away into cupboards and drawers and forgot all about lunch.'

'Why don't you get something now?' she suggested, leading the way to the buffet tables. Picking up a plate and some napkin-wrapped cutlery, she handed them to him, snatching her hand away when their fingers accidentally touched. 'It all looks delicious,' she declared but Sean could hear the quaver in her voice and didn't know whether to be pleased or sorry. Obviously, Molly wasn't as indifferent to him as she was making out.

'Aren't you having anything?' he asked, trying to batten down the rush of emotions that hit him at that idea. Did he want her to feel something for him or not? Quite frankly, he couldn't decide or, rather, he chose not to arrive at a conclusion. It was too risky to do that, to examine his feelings and come up with an answer that might only complicate matters even further.

'How about some of this smoked salmon?' he suggested, spearing a morsel on the end of his fork. He offered it to her and smiled, praying that she couldn't tell how ambivalent he felt, how confused. He wanted her so much but he couldn't have her unless he broke his vow to Claire. And the thought tore him in two. 'You always loved smoked salmon, didn't you?' he added inanely because he needed to keep talking, otherwise he might do something really stupid. He couldn't promise Molly the earth when it wasn't his to give.

'Yes, I did.' She looked back at him and Sean could see a host of memories in her eyes, recollections of all the other times when they had eaten together, laughed together, got to know one another's likes and dislikes. When she leant forward and delicately closed her lips around the morsel of food Sean felt the blood surge through his veins. There in a room filled with people laughing and enjoying themselves, he and Molly stood alone, set apart from everyone else by their memories.

He knew then that he would always remember this moment because it was when he realised that he wouldn't have changed what had happened between them even if he could have done. That time he had spent with Molly was far too precious; he needed the memory of it far too much. It was the one bright and shining period to come out of all these long years of darkness and despair.

Molly could taste the savoury tang of the salmon on her tongue and shuddered. She wasn't sure why she had done that—leant forward and accepted the treat Sean had offered her. The action smacked of an intimacy that she knew she shouldn't encourage and yet she had still done it, hadn't she? Why? Did she want to experience their former closeness once more when it would mean risking getting hurt all over again? Surely she wasn't so foolish as to imagine that this time it would be different, that this time Sean would want her to remain in his life for good? After what she had learned about Claire, the possibility of that happening was zero.

Picking up a plate, Molly started to fill it with delicacies even though the thought of actually eating any of it made her feel sick. However, it was something to do, something normal and stress-free, and that was what she needed desperately. Sean had loaded his plate with a selection of goodies and was looking round for somewhere to sit down; he nodded towards a couple of vacant chairs in the corner near the window.

'Let's go over there while we eat this little lot,' he suggested, leading the way.

Molly followed him in silence, half afraid that all the thoughts whizzing around inside her head would somehow pop out into the open. It wasn't Sean's fault if he could never love her like he had loved Claire and it would be wrong to make him feel guilty about it. Sitting down, she spread the paper napkin over her lap then balanced her plate on her knees, hoping that she would manage to eat some of the food she had collected.

'Mmm, this is delicious. Did you pick up one of these?'

Sean showed her a tiny pastry tart filled with cream cheese and prawns and Molly shook her head then swallowed as a wave of nausea suddenly struck her.

'No? Then have this one. I picked up two, greedy guts that I am, so it's only fair that I share them with you.' He went to pop the tartlet on her plate but Molly pushed his hand away.

'No! I… I don't like prawns,' she muttered, using the first excuse she could come up with to explain why she'd been so abrupt.

'Really?' Sean frowned, his dark brows drawing together as he stared at her in surprise. 'Since when? You used to love prawns. Why, they were your favourite sandwich filling. Whenever I asked you what you wanted from the canteen, it was always a prawn mayonnaise sandwich.'

'I probably ate so many that I sickened myself of them,' Molly said snappily, wishing that he didn't have such excellent recall. Was he going to dredge up every itty-bitty scrap of information about her? she thought sourly, then realised how contrary she was being. The fact that Sean remembered which sandwiches she had liked should have been a boost to her ego. It proved that he hadn't simply dismissed her from his mind the minute he had left Dalverston, as she had imagined.

The thought was unsettling, far too unsettling to explore at that moment. Molly concentrated on her supper and managed to eat at least some of the food on her plate. Sean was tucking in with gusto and sighed with contentment when the last morsel had disappeared.

'That was delicious. Best food I've eaten in days. I love living in the cottage but I haven't quite got to grips with the Aga yet.' He groaned. 'I didn't think it was possible to burn water but I managed it. Or rather I burnt the potatoes that were supposed to be boiling in it!'

Molly laughed as well, thinking how handsome he looked as he sat there, his deep blue eyes filled with self-mocking laughter. Sean had never taken himself too seriously. He had such an easy manner about him that both staff and patients alike were always comfortable when he was around. He was very different in that respect from Adam Humphreys. Adam tended to stand very much on ceremony—he was the doctor and he wanted everyone to remember it too. She couldn't imagine Adam laughing at himself like that and it was the last thought she needed when, every time she compared the two men, Sean came out on top.

'You need some lessons,' she said, hurriedly steering her thoughts down a less dangerous track.

'If that's an offer, then yes, please. Both me and my poor stomach would be eternally grateful if you could give me a few tips on how to master the wretched thing.'

'Oh, I…um…' Molly floundered, caught completely off-guard by the suggestion.

'How about tomorrow morning? You're off this weekend and I'm on a late on Saturday so it would be perfect.'

He looked so hopeful that Molly found the refusal dying on her lips. After all, what harm could there be in giving him some pointers about the art of Aga cooking?

'All right. Around ten, shall we say?'

'Brilliant!' He rolled his eyes lasciviously. 'Oh, I can't wait to cook myself a meal that doesn't taste—or smell—as though it's been cremated!'

Molly laughed. Even though he was hamming it up for all he was worth, it was good to know that she could help him at least with regard to his cooking skills. As for the rest, well, there was very little she could do about that.

Thankfully, there was no time to dwell on that thought as the best man called for silence just then and asked everyone to raise their glasses to toast the happy couple. Once that was done, music began to play and Bert and Doris took to the floor in a stately and surprisingly accomplished waltz. Other people started to join in and Molly jumped when Sean touched her lightly on the arm.

'Fancy a go?' He grinned at her. 'I can't promise not to tread on your toes but I'll give it my best shot.'

'Why not?' she said because it seemed churlish to refuse when everyone else was dancing. She followed him onto the dance floor, steeling herself when he took her in his arms. Even though he was holding her at arm's length, it wasn't easy to ignore the powerful attraction of his body. They completed a full circuit of the floor, their steps fitting so perfectly that there was no danger of him trampling on her toes. Tossing back her hair, Molly treated him to a mock-fierce stare.

'I think you were spinning me a line, Sean Fitzgerald. You're an excellent dancer so what was that rubbish about not treading on my toes all about?'

'Because on the few occasions when I've attempted to dance like this before, I've left my partner with multiple bruises.' He twirled her round, bending her backwards over his arm and leering comically down at her like some fifth-rate gigolo. 'You, my lovely, have inspired me!'

Molly laughed as he pulled her back up. It was such a load of nonsense and yet she couldn't help enjoying the way he made everything seem like such fun. When the music changed to a much faster rhythm this time, they remained on the floor, simply enjoying the chance to be together in such an undemanding fashion. They were having fun: it was as simple as that. And if she was having more fun because she was with Sean then Molly refused to think about it. It was easier this way. Less complicated. Less painful.

Sean collected Molly's coat from the cloakroom, wishing that the evening didn't have to end. It had been a wonderful night and he wanted it to carry on but everything had to come to an end at some point. Just for a second he found himself refuting that idea. It didn't need to end if he didn't choose to let it. Tonight could be the start of a whole lot more wonderful nights. All he had to do was make the decision and the future could be his. He could move on with Molly at his side...

If he left Claire behind.

The thought sent a stab of guilt through his guts. It was hard to hide how upset he felt as he went back to find Molly and helped her on with her coat. Bert and Doris were standing by the door, seeing their guests out, and he and Molly kissed them both and wished them well before they left. It was freezing cold outside, their breath clouding like cartoon speech bubbles as they hurried to his car. Sean zapped the locks then turned to help Molly into the seat, cursing softly when the car keys slipped out of his numb fingers.

'I'll get them.' Molly bent down to retrieve the keys at the same moment as he did and their heads collided. 'Ouch!' she exclaimed, straightening up.

'I am so sorry!' Sean declared. He turned her so that she was facing the light from a nearby streetlamp and grimaced. 'Oh, dear. It looks as though you're going to end up with a lump on your forehead.'

'Not to worry.' She ran a tentative finger over her forehead and groaned. 'Ooh, that hurts!'

'We'll put some ice on it as soon as we get you home.' Sean helped her into the car then climbed behind the wheel, feeling dreadful about what had happened. It only took ten minutes to reach her house and he was out of the car and standing beside her door before she could protest. 'No. I am not letting you go without at least trying to make amends for my clumsiness.' He gave her a severe look. 'I mean, what kind of a doctor would I be if I left some poor injured soul to her own devices?'

'It's just a bump, Sean.' She rolled her eyes as she slid out of the car. 'It's not as though my head is in any danger of dropping off!'

'You can't be too careful with head injuries,' he said, adopting his firmest tone. He locked the car and followed her up the path to the front door. 'Are there any ice cubes in your freezer?' he asked once they were inside.

'No. The best I can offer you is a bag of frozen peas.' Molly led the way into her tiny kitchen and opened the freezer door. She handed him a bag of peas. 'Do these meet with your requirements, Dr Fitzgerald?' she asked a shade sarcastically.

'They'll do.' Sean whipped a tea towel off the rack and wrapped the bag of peas in it then told her to sit down, ignoring her huff of annoyance. Maybe he was going over the top but he intended to make up for having injured her even if she didn't appreciate it. Taking care of Molly was just something he needed to do.

The thought that he wouldn't be able to look after her once he left Dalverston whizzed through his brain but he blanked it out. He pressed the makeshift ice pack against her temple and felt her flinch. 'Sorry, did that hurt?' he asked, bending to look at her.

'No. It's just that it's so cold it made me jump.'

Her voice sounded husky and Sean felt a ripple of awareness spread throughout his body. Was it the coldness or his nearness that was making her sound so on edge? he wondered as he continued to hold the ice pack against her temple. The thought that it might be the latter made him shudder too and he strove to get a grip on himself, not an easy thing to do in the circumstances. Standing this close to her, he could smell the delicate floral fragrance of her perfume and his heart ran wild. All of a sudden it wasn't enough to minister to her this way. He wanted to touch her far more intimately, to run his hands over her and let them relearn the luscious curves, the dips and hollows, to lose himself in the wonder of her delectable body. But should he? Could he? Or would he simply be storing up a whole load of heartache for both him and Molly? How could he take what she could give him when he had nothing to offer her in return?

Molly could feel the tension swirling around them and swallowed the sudden knot in her throat. She knew what was happening and had a very good idea what Sean was thinking too. Would he act upon these feelings that filled the air? Would he take her in his arms and make love to her, because that was where this was leading? But was it what she wanted, *really* wanted, when she knew in her heart that it could only end in yet more heartache? At the end of the day, it wouldn't change anything. He would still be in love with Claire, no matter what they did tonight.

The thought brought her back down to earth with a bump. Pushing his hand away, she stood up. It was hard to control her emotions but she refused to make a fool of herself again. Maybe she did want him to make love to her but she couldn't bear the thought of how she would feel afterwards. When he left Dalverston and left her.

'I think it's time you went, don't you?' she said, hearing the strain in her voice but unable to do anything about it.

'Yes.' He put the makeshift compress on the table and took a deep breath. 'I'm sorry, Molly—'

'Don't!' Molly gave a sharp downward thrust of her hand, unable to deal with the thought of him apologising for what had so nearly happened. It would take very little to change her mind and that was something she mustn't do. Until Sean was free of the past then he wouldn't be free to love her or any other woman.

He didn't say anything more as he turned and walked down the hall. Molly followed him out, pausing when he stopped and turned to face her. There was such sadness in his eyes that her heart ached but she couldn't afford to weaken. What it came down to was one simple fact: Sean could never love her while he was in love with someone else.

'I think it's probably best if we forget about tomorrow.' He gave her a quick grin but it was for show rather than a true expression of his feelings. That he was as upset as she was wasn't in any doubt and Molly's aching heart ached all the more. 'I shall muddle through and master that wretched cooker somehow.'

'You will. It's not exactly rocket science, is it?' Molly did her best to play her part in the proceedings; however, the catch in her voice somewhat spoiled her efforts.

'It isn't.' He gave a small shrug then started to open the door before he suddenly swung back to face her. 'I wish things could be different, Molly. Really I do!'

Molly had no time to react when he pulled her into his arms and kissed her. Maybe she should have pushed him away, remonstrated with him, done *something* to show it wasn't what she wanted, but she was incapable of doing anything at that moment. His lips clung to hers, demanding a response she was powerless to refuse. The kiss might have lasted seconds or hours—she had no idea which it was—but she was trembling when Sean let her go. He didn't say a word as he opened the front door, didn't look back as he got into his car and drove away, but she understood. If he had spoken to her or looked at her then he couldn't have left. He would have had to stay.

Molly was trembling as she closed the door and went and sat down on the stairs. She could tell herself until the moon turned blue that she was glad she hadn't let him make love to her tonight but it would be a lie. She knew that and, what was more, Sean knew it too.

CHAPTER TWELVE

THE NEXT COUPLE of weeks passed in a blur. Sean offered to work extra shifts whenever they were short-staffed and managed to fill up his time to the exclusion of everything else. He did fit in some Christmas shopping on a rare day off, buying presents for his parents as well as some chocolates for the rest of the team in A&E, but that was the full extent of his preparations. Christmas and New Year were always difficult times; they brought it home to him how different his life might have been if Claire hadn't died, although, strangely, he found it less painful this year. The thought that he was moving on, and that it had a lot to do with how he felt about Molly, filled him with guilt.

Although he saw Molly most days in work, he had the distinct impression that she was going out of her way to avoid him. Although they lived only a short distance apart, he never ever bumped into her in the street. He hadn't even seen her driving into work, which struck him as very odd, seeing as they must have driven along the same route. When the thought occurred to him that

she might be spending more time with Adam Humphreys, possibly even sleeping at Humphreys' house, it
didn't exactly fill Sean with cheer. The sooner his stint
at Dalverston was over, the better!

Molly had managed to cram some much-needed Christmas shopping in after work and had parcelled up the
presents she intended to send home to her parents and
younger sister. She was rostered to work all over the
Christmas period so she wouldn't be able to give them
their presents in person this year.

She had been due to have New Year off but Joyce's
accident had caused problems with the time sheets and
she ended up volunteering to work then as well. Although Joyce was still in ICU, she was making some
progress and the neurosurgical team were cautiously
optimistic. Molly popped in most days to check on her
and have a word with Ted, who was constantly at her
bedside. His devotion was touching and Molly was sure
that if the power of love could affect the outcome then
her friend had a very good chance of recovering.

The thought naturally reminded her of Sean but
then again he was rarely out of her mind. He was the
first thought that popped into her head when she woke
each morning and his was the last face she saw before
she fell asleep. She had taken to avoiding him, even
going to the extent of taking a circuitous route when she
drove into work. What had almost happened that night
after Bert and Doris's wedding reception had come as

a timely warning about how vulnerable she was. Whenever Adam asked her out, she always accepted even though she found him extremely dull company. The fact that their relationship had never moved beyond a courteous peck on the cheek was another indication that there was no spark there, at least on her part. No, Adam definitely didn't ring any bells. Not like Sean had done. And still did.

In an effort to distract herself, Molly packed as much as possible into each and every day. When she wasn't working, she was either cooking or cleaning. Her house sparkled from top to bottom while the fridge and freezer were crammed to overflowing with goodies. Why, if an entire army had descended on her this Christmas, she could have fed them! By the time Christmas Eve arrived there wasn't space for another morsel of food in the house.

She was rostered to work that night but arrived early as she had volunteered to sing in the staff choir. They had decided to dress up in the uniforms that had been worn by nurses during the First World War and there was much hilarity as they donned the floor-length dresses and heavy woollen capes. The caps were the most difficult to master; it took Molly half a dozen attempts before she managed to anchor the starched folds of cotton to her hair and even then she wasn't confident that it would stay on her head. The men had opted to wear soldiers' uniforms and a cheer went up when they marched into the canteen, resplendent in their khaki kit. Molly hadn't realised until that moment that Sean would be with them and her heart leapt when she spotted his tall, muscular figure standing at the back of the group. She couldn't help thinking how impressive he looked in his uniform.

They set off around the hospital, stopping at each ward to sing a selection of well-known carols. The staff dimmed the lights so that they sang in the glow given off by the lanterns they were carrying. It was very atmospheric and Molly noticed several people wiping away a tear or two. By the time they finished doing the rounds, it was declared a resounding success. Molly changed back into her usual attire and made her way to A&E. Sean was already there and he smiled when she went over to the desk.

'Back to normal, I see. Although I have to admit that your previous outfit was very fetching, especially that cap. It was a miracle of engineering!'

'I...erm...thank you.' Molly felt the blush start at her throat and work its way upwards. Reaching over the desk, she snagged the daily report sheet and bent over it, hoping to hide her embarrassment. Just because Sean had paid her a compliment, it wasn't an excuse to start behaving like a giddy teenager.

'Mind you, fetching though the dresses were, I don't know how the women coped with those long skirts. It must have been a nightmare trying to keep them clean.'

'It must.'

Molly gave him a quick smile then went to check

what everyone was doing. There were three nurses working that night, including herself, plus Sean and a locum doctor. Once she was sure that everyone knew what they were doing she went back to the desk, relieved to find that Sean had disappeared. So long as they stuck to work then everything would fine, she assured herself. It was when they got onto more personal issues that the problems started.

The night started off slowly enough and it looked as though it was going to stay that way too. Molly took her break at eleven o'clock and was in the staffroom making herself a cup of coffee when she heard the emergency telephone start to ring. Abandoning her drink, she hurried back to the unit to see what was going on. Sean had taken the call and her heart sank when she saw how grim he looked as he hung up.

'What's happened?' she asked, going straight over to him.

'A private plane has crashed onto the old brewery in the town centre. Apparently, it was heading to Barton airport near Manchester but the pilot reported that they were experiencing engine problems.'

'Oh, no! They renovated the brewery a couple of years ago and turned it into luxury apartments. Heaven only knows how many people are living there now.'

'Incident control is liaising with the police to try and establish that. It's not going to be easy, mind you. At this time of the year a lot of folk could have gone away to visit relatives or even be on holiday.'

'It's going to be a major task,' Molly agreed. 'So what's the plan? Are you declaring it a major incident and calling in extra staff to deal with the casualties?'

'I don't think I have a choice.' Sean grimaced. 'On Christmas Eve too. I really will be popular.'

Molly left him to speak to the switchboard, who would phone everyone on the list of staff who were down to attend when something like this happened. She called the rest of the team into the office and quickly explained what had happened. By the time that was done, Sean had finished and came to find her.

'Incident control has asked us to send a team to the site. You and I will go, obviously, but we could do with another nurse plus a doctor to make up our numbers. Who do you suggest? I know Steph is on her way in but I can't take her. Apart from the fact that she hasn't done the necessary training, it will leave us short in here.'

'Jayne will be the best person to accompany us,' Molly replied, referring to Jayne Leonard, one of their most experienced staff nurses. She frowned. 'I'm not sure about another doctor— Oh, how about Mac— James MacIntyre, remember him? He used to work here. He's not only done the necessary training but he dealt with all sorts of incidents when he was working overseas for that aid agency. The experience he's gained from that could be very useful.'

'Great! I remember Mac from when I last worked here. He was a first rate doctor too.' Sean frowned. 'How come he doesn't work here any longer?'

'He's moved to the new paediatric A&E unit. He's senior registrar and, rumour has it, he's tipped to be their next consultant when their current boss retires next year,' Molly explained, leading the way to the store room.

'Really?' Sean unhooked a waterproof suit off its peg and started to pull on the trousers. 'I didn't think that Mac was the sort to settle down in one place for very long.'

'He's changed a lot since he and Bella got married,' Molly told him and laughed. 'They have a little girl now—she must be almost a year old, in fact. And, according to Bella, Mac is a doting father!'

'Well, that's great,' Sean said, trying to ignore the pang of regret that pierced his heart. He had ruled out the idea of having children after what had happened with Claire, yet all of a sudden he found himself envying the other man. How wonderful it must be to have a wife and a child to love and cherish.

He drove the thought from his mind as he gathered together everything they might need. An incident like this could create all sorts of problems and he wanted to be as prepared as it was possible to be. Once he had made arrangements with the switchboard to contact Mac, he led the way out to the front where a rapid response car was waiting to ferry them to the old brewery. Ambulances had already been dispatched although more could be called in from neighbouring health authorities if they were needed.

It took them less than ten minutes to reach the brewery and Sean's heart sank when he saw the state of the place. The plane had struck the roof of the building, causing it, along with several floors beneath, to collapse. The fire department was pumping foam onto the burning jet fuel but the right hand side of the building was ablaze. There were groups of people dotted about, some standing and others lying on the ground. The place looked like a war zone and he realised that his most pressing task was to get everyone organised.

'Right, guys, gather round.' He waited until everyone had assembled at the side of the car park. 'I doubt if we'll be allowed inside the building until they have got that fire under control so we'll deal with the people out here first.' He turned to Molly. 'If you and Jayne can sort out the most seriously injured that would be a huge help. I'll check with the incident commander to see if they've managed to find somewhere to house the casualties. Then we can round them up and get them away from here.'

'Will do.'

Molly picked up her backpack before she and Jayne hurried away. Sean watched her go and sighed as he found his mind skipping back to what he had been thinking earlier. There was no doubt at all that Molly would make the most wonderful mother but they definitely wouldn't be his children that she gave birth to.

It was an effort to force the thought from his mind but he knew that he couldn't afford to waste any time

in getting everything organised. Once he was sure that
everyone knew what they were doing, he went to find
the incident commander. Fortunately, she had already
arranged for a local church hall to be opened up and
used as a temporary field hospital so within a very
short time the first casualties were being taken in there.
Molly was kneeling beside a young woman when Sean
arrived. She shook her head when he asked her if she
needed anything.

'No, we're fine. Just a few cuts and bruises, I'm
pleased to say.'

She squeezed the girl's hand and Sean felt his throat
close up when he saw the compassion on her face.
Whether it was the fact that his mind had been skitter-
ing this way and that, he had no idea, but he couldn't
help feeling touched. Molly really cared about the people they treated—it wasn't just an act. She was such a
genuinely kind and generous person yet he had treated
her appallingly. If he achieved nothing else while he was
in Dalverston then at the very least he had to make his
peace with her. The thought of her thinking badly of
him for the rest of her days was more than he could bear.

Molly finished patching up the young woman and left
her in the care of her boyfriend. Sean was attending to
a man who had been struck by some falling masonry
when the roof had caved in. He had suffered multiple
rib fractures which had resulted in a flail chest—a condition whereby the damaged section of the chest wall

was sucked in when the patient breathed in and moved out when he exhaled. This type of injury could lead to respiratory failure and Sean was in the process of strapping the patient's chest to support the damaged section before the paramedics rushed him off to hospital. He shook his head as he watched the crew wheel the trolley out of the hall.

'He's going to need artificial ventilation until those ribs heal. I've seen a couple of flail chests before but none as bad as that.'

'Thankfully, he doesn't have far to go to reach the hospital,' Molly said quietly.

Sean nodded. 'You're right. He's lucky in that respect, although I doubt if he feels very lucky. Apparently, he only moved into the building last week. His apartment is one of those in the section that's burning so he's lost everything.'

'At least he wasn't in the apartment,' Molly said firmly. 'Things can be replaced but people can't.'

'True.'

He gave her a quick smile before he turned away but she had seen the sadness in his eyes. Was he thinking about Claire and how he would never be able to replace her? Although he hadn't come out and actually said so, it was obvious that he was still very much in love with Claire.

It was a painful thought. Molly had great difficulty setting it aside as she attended to several more casualties. Mac had arrived now and he and Sean were busy dealing with a woman who had suffered a severe abdominal injury when one of the fire crew appeared and hurried over to them. Molly frowned as she watched them confer. It was obvious that something had happened.

Sean came over to her as soon as the fireman had left. 'I need your help, Molly, but I have to warn you that it could be risky, so you must say if you feel that you don't want to do it.'

'Why? What's happened?' she asked.

'The search and rescue team have located a woman trapped in one of the first floor apartments. The problem is that they have only managed to clear a very small area to get to her—more like a tunnel is how the fireman described it. It's not wide enough for any of their men to get through and they daren't risk enlarging it in case the floor above caves in. It's just possible that you might be able to get up there if you're willing to give it a shot.'

'Of course,' she said immediately. 'Have they spoken to the woman and do they know if she's been injured?'

'Yes.' He grimaced. 'Her name is Karen Archer and, although she isn't injured, she is pregnant. The baby was due at the end of January but she thinks she might be having labour pains.'

'Oh, dear. That doesn't sound good, does it? The sooner I take a look at her the better.'

Molly hurried to the door, pausing only long enough to tell Jayne what was happening. Sean led her over to the officer in charge of the search and rescue team and explained that she was willing to try to reach the woman. Molly nodded when the man explained the situation once more, emphasising how difficult it was going to be to get to the apartment.

'I understand,' she said, her heart thumping. 'I'd still like to give it a shot, though.'

'Are you sure, Molly?' Sean asked softly as the officer went off to speak to one of his team. He took hold of her hand and gently squeezed it. 'Nobody will blame you if you decide not to go ahead.'

'We can't leave that poor woman on her own if the baby's coming.' She dredged up a rather wobbly smile. 'I'll be fine, Sean. Don't worry about me.'

'I can't help it. I couldn't bear to think of anything happening to you, Molly.'

He gave her fingers another quick squeeze then let her go when the officer came back. Molly forced herself to concentrate as he ran through a list of instructions aimed at keeping her safe. She knew it was important that she listened to what he was saying but it wasn't easy to remain focused. *Sean cared about her, really cared about her.* It had been clear from the tone of his voice that he had been telling her the truth just now and she wasn't sure what to make of it. All she knew was that it changed things, gave her a reason to hope, although she wasn't ready to admit exactly what she was hoping for. That was a step too far. Or, at least, it was at the moment.

CHAPTER THIRTEEN

THE SITUATION WAS even worse than Sean had expected. Once they were inside the building, it soon became clear just how much structural damage had occurred. The stairs leading to the upper floors had collapsed, leaving behind a pile of rubble in their place. The fire crew had managed to clear a narrow passageway which Molly would have to scramble through to reach the first floor. Although sturdy metal props had been erected to help support the upper section of the building, he was very aware that it could collapse at any second. The thought of Molly risking her life was more than he could bear and he drew her aside.

'I can't allow you to go up there, Molly. It's far too risky.'

'I have to go. We can't leave that poor woman on her own while her baby is born.' She shrugged. 'I'll be fine, Sean. After all, they wouldn't allow me to try it if they thought I'd be putting myself in danger, would they?'

Sean knew she was right, although it wasn't much

comfort. He shook his head. 'I still don't like the idea. If anyone's going up there then it has to be me.'

'How? You're too big to get through that gap, Sean. Why, even I'm going to have difficulty so you definitely won't make it.'

'I suppose so.' Sean sighed as he was forced to concede defeat. 'All right, but you're to promise me that you will turn back if you encounter any problems.'

'Cross my heart.' She drew an imaginary cross over her heart with her fingertip and he laughed.

'You do realise that I'm going to hold you to that, Sister Daniels?'

'Of course!'

She treated him to a smile before one of the crew came over to ask if she was ready. Sean sucked in a tiny breath of air, feeling ripples of heat running through him. Molly had smiled at him the way she had used to do and it felt wonderful to be on the receiving end of all that warmth again.

There was no time to dwell on the thought, however. One of the search and rescue team was attaching Molly to a safety harness. Once he was sure that she understood how it worked, he handed her a two-way radio receiver and led her to the bottom of the gap, showing her where to place her foot to begin her ascent. Sean's hands clenched as he watched her start to scramble up over the rubble. The surface was very unstable but somehow she managed to find the necessary hand and footholds. Within seconds she disappeared from sight, leaving him feeling more anxious than ever. She was on her own now and he didn't like that idea, not when he wanted to be there to protect her.

Sean froze as the full impact of that thought hit him squarely in the chest. He wanted to protect Molly from harm and not just for now either. He wanted to be there for her for ever and ever more.

Molly was out of breath by the time she made it to the top of the passageway. It had been a difficult climb but, thankfully, the first floor appeared to be relatively un-damaged. She unfastened the safety harness then picked her way around the chunks of plaster that had fallen from the ceiling until she came to the apartment. The door was wide open and she hurried inside, her heart sinking when she found the woman slumped on the living room floor.

'Hi! It's Karen, isn't it? I'm Molly and I'm a nurse. So how are you doing?' she said, kneeling beside her. She was somewhat older than Molly had expected, prob-ably in her early forties, and it was obvious how scared she was.

'I think I'm in labour.' She looked up and there were tears in her eyes. 'Please don't let my baby die. We've waited such a long time to have a child of our own and I couldn't bear it if anything happened to it now.'

'Nothing is going to happen to you or your baby,' Molly said firmly, knowing this wasn't the time to worry about the ethics of making such a statement.

Karen needed all the reassurance she could give her if she was to get through this ordeal. 'Let's make you more comfortable for starters. Can you stand up if I help you?'

'I'll try.'

'Great.' Molly put her arm around her and managed to get her to her feet and onto the sofa. 'I need to examine you to see if you are actually in labour, if that's all right.'

Karen nodded, her face scrunching up with pain. Molly suspected it was labour pains but she still needed to check that it wasn't a false alarm first. She quickly removed Karen's underclothes, hiding her dismay when she discovered that the woman was fully dilated. There was little doubt that the baby was going to make his or her appearance very shortly.

'You're definitely in labour,' she told her. 'I've brought everything we need with me so I'll just get ready. Have you been to any antenatal classes?'

'Oh, yes. Mike—that's my husband—and I have done them all. Breathing and relaxation techniques, what happens during the delivery and afterwards.' Karen gave a slightly hysterical laugh. 'We thought we were completely prepared for the birth, but the one thing we didn't foresee was that this would happen!'

'No wonder.' Molly laughed. 'Where is your husband, by the way?'

'He went to fill up the car with petrol to make sure he wouldn't run out over Christmas,' Karen explained. 'I wish he was here. I'd feel a lot happier if he was around to talk me through all those breathing techniques we learned.'

'I'm sure you would but we'll manage fine.' Molly squeezed Karen's hand. 'The fact that you've done the classes will be a big help.'

'But the baby is still going to be born early,' Karen said anxiously.

'Yes, but only by a few weeks so the lungs should be fully developed,' Molly assured her. 'Right, I'm just going to fetch what I need and then listen to your baby's heartbeat.'

Opening her bag, she took out the emergency birthing pack that was part of their standard equipment. Fortunately, she'd done a refresher course earlier in the year on delivering a baby so she had few qualms in that respect. However, delivering a child in the confines of the A&E department was very different from what was happening here. Just for a moment, she found herself wishing that Sean was there with her before she sighed. Sean wasn't here and she would have to get through this on her own. It would be good practice for the future because, once Sean completed his contract, he would leave Dalverston and she doubted if he would ever come back again.

The time seemed to pass with excruciating slowness. Sean found himself continually checking his watch, unable to believe that mere minutes had passed when it felt like hours since Molly had disappeared into the

upper reaches of the building. What was happening up
there? Had Molly found the woman? Or had she en-
countered some sort of a problem? His mind raced over
a dozen different possibilities, each worse than the one
before, and he groaned. He would drive himself crazy
if he carried on this way!

The crackle of the radio receiver cut through his
thoughts. Sean's heart lifted when he heard Molly's
voice issuing from the speaker as she asked to speak to
him. He took the receiver with a nod of thanks, overcome by relief.

'How's it going?' he asked, trying not to let her know
how worried he had been. 'Have you found the woman?'

'Yes, and she's definitely in labour. She's fully dilated so it shouldn't be long before the baby arrives. I've
checked its heart rate and everything seems to be fine
but can you arrange for an ambulance to be standing
by just in case anything happens at the last moment?'

'Of course.' He paused but the words had to be said,
no matter what repercussions they might cause. 'Be
careful, won't you, Molly? I don't want you putting
yourself at risk. You're too important to me.'

'Am I?' she said so softly that he had to strain to
hear her.

'Yes.' He took a deep breath but it was time he admitted the truth to himself as much as to her. 'You always were.'

There was no time to say anything else as there were
too many other issues to deal with. Sean handed over

the radio while one of the crew ran through the emergency evacuation procedure with Molly. He listened while the other man explained what would happen once the baby was delivered but it was difficult to concentrate when his thoughts were in such turmoil. Maybe he had been wrong to tell Molly that he cared but he needed to set matters straight once and for all. If it weren't for that vow he had made then he knew that he would never have let her go.

Sean knew it was the wrong time to think about such matters. Forcing his mind back to the current crisis, he headed outside to arrange for an ambulance to be standing by. He had just reached the door when a shout went up and the next moment the ceiling started to collapse. Huge chunks of debris rained down on them as he and the crew scrambled to safety. He came to a halt in the car park, bending double as he tried to clear the dust from his lungs. The air was thick with it so that it took a while before he could see what had happened and his heart seized up at the sight that met him. The entire front of the building had collapsed, leaving what remained of the upper floors suspended in mid-air. And, somewhere inside that wreckage, Molly was trapped.

Molly had no time to do anything when the building started to shake. She simply knelt down beside the sofa and gripped tight hold of Karen's hand. There was a tremendous roar, like an express train rushing through a tunnel, and then silence. Clouds of dust were swirling around them, making it impossible to see across the room, and she waited until it had settled before she stood up.

'Where are you going? Don't leave me!' Karen grabbed hold of her hand in panic and Molly paused.

'I'm just going to see what's happened. I'll only be a second.'

She eased her hand free and picked her way around the chunks of masonry that littered the living room floor. The apartment was a mess but it was only when she reached the bedroom that she discovered the full extent of the damage. There was a gaping hole now where the front wall should have been. She didn't dare go any closer because the floor was tilted at an angle but, from what she could tell, it appeared that the entire front section of the building had collapsed.

Molly's heart was racing as she made her way back to the living room to find the radio receiver, hoping that someone would be able to tell her how long it would take before they got her and Karen out. However, one glance at the shattered remains of the handset soon put paid to that idea. All she could do now was pray that help would arrive before the rest of the building collapsed as well.

'Some bits of the front wall have collapsed,' she explained as she crouched down beside the sofa. She dredged up a smile, deciding that it would be better to play down the true extent of the damage. The last thing she wanted was to cause Karen any more stress. 'I'm sure they'll sort it out so let's concentrate on you and this baby, shall we? Have you decided on a name yet?'

'Mike and I decided that we didn't want to know what sex it was—we preferred to wait and see when it was born. So it's Holly if it's a girl and Nicholas if it's a boy,' Karen replied and then groaned. 'Oh! Here we go again.'

Molly checked the time but there was no doubt that Karen's contractions were coming closer together, a sure sign that the birth was imminent. She held Karen's hand until the pain eased and nodded. 'You're doing really well. It shouldn't be long before your baby is born so what I need now is something to wrap him or her in. Do you have a blanket handy?'

'Everything's packed in that green case near the window in our bedroom.' Karen's face screwed up as she focused on getting through the next contraction.

Molly bit back a sigh because the case, along with everything else at that side of the bedroom, was now in the car park.

'I'm afraid I can't get at it at the moment so we'll have to use something else, like a towel, for instance. That would be fine.'

'Oh. Well, there's clean towels in the bathroom cupboard.'

'Great.' Molly hurriedly fetched a couple of towels and placed them on a nearby chair. She checked Karen once more. 'The baby's head is crowning, so you're nearly there.'

She carefully supported the baby's head as it emerged, checking that the umbilical cord wasn't wrapped around its neck, which could prevent it breathing. Then first one shoulder and then the other were delivered. The rest of the body slid out in a rush as the child began to cry lustily.

Molly laughed in relief. 'Congratulations! You have a beautiful little boy who, from the sound of it, has a fine pair of lungs.' She cleaned the baby, tied and cut his umbilical cord, then wrapped him in a towel and handed him to Karen. 'Well done. You were absolutely marvellous, especially as you didn't have the benefit of any pain relief.'

'It doesn't matter,' Karen murmured, staring at her baby son in awe. 'It was worth all the pain to be able to hold my own child in my arms at last.'

Molly left them to get to know one another while she tidied up. Once the afterbirth had been expelled, she left the apartment and gingerly made her way towards where she had entered the building. There was no sign of the passageway that the crew had cleared for her, only a heap of rubble. It looked as though they were trapped up here until help arrived. Once again she found herself wishing that Sean was there with her before she drove the thought from her mind. It would be stupid to allow herself to become dependent on him.

Sean had never pulled rank before but he had no qualms about doing so now. The rescue crew had set up a long ladder with a cage on the top and were proposing to enter the building to search for Molly and Karen by using that. He shook his head when the officer in charge explained once more that his men were all trained in the use of first aid.

'No, it's not enough,' he said shortly, determined that if anyone was going into the building, it was going to be him. The thought of having to stand here and wait any longer for news was more than he could handle. He needed to find Molly and make sure that she was all right. He would never forgive himself if anything had happened to her.

It was hard to deal with that thought but he needed to convince the other man it was essential that he was included as part of the team. 'There's a woman up there who is about to give birth under the most difficult circumstances. Add to that the fact that the baby is premature and you can see why it's vital that I go with your men.'

The officer obviously saw the logic of what he was saying. Sean sighed in relief when he was briskly told to get kitted up. One of the crew attached him to a safety harness before he was helped into the cage along with two other men. Nobody said anything as the ladder slowly rose; Sean suspected that everyone was feeling as anxious as he was. However, this wasn't only a rescue mission for him. He was trying to save the woman he loved.

His breath caught painfully but there was no point

trying to deny how he felt any longer. He loved Molly and he wanted to be with her, but could he do so when it would mean breaking his promise to Claire? He sucked in a deep breath of air. Somehow he had to find a solution to this dilemma because one thing was certain: he couldn't face the thought of a future without Molly.

CHAPTER FOURTEEN

MOLLY COULD FEEL her fear rising as the minutes ticked past. How long had it been since the front wall of the building had collapsed? Ten minutes? Fifteen? Twenty, even? Surely something should be happening by now.

She went to the bedroom door but she could see very little from where she stood. She stepped tentatively into the room then stopped abruptly when she felt the floor give beneath her feet. She backed out of the door, her heart racing nineteen to the dozen as she realised just how serious the situation was. The whole building could collapse at any moment from the look of it and she, Karen and the baby would be trapped inside.

It was hard not to show her concern as she went to check on Karen. She was cradling baby Nicholas to her breast when Molly went into the sitting room and she looked hopefully up at her.

'Has the rescue team arrived?'

'Not yet, but I'm sure they won't be long now,' Molly told her, crossing her fingers behind her back. Maybe it was a lie but it was better than worrying the poor soul to death by telling her the truth. 'How are you doing? Do you feel all right?'

'Fine.' Karen smiled down at the baby. 'I have this little fellow to look after and he's my main concern now.'

'He's beautiful,' Molly said truthfully. 'And, what's more, he's probably one of the first babies to be born on Christmas Day this year. That makes him even more special.'

'We certainly won't forget his birthday!' Karen declared, laughing. She sobered abruptly when there was a loud crash from the direction of the hall. 'Oh, what was that?'

'I'll go and see.'

Molly hurried to the door, her heart sinking when she saw that a large hole had appeared in the hall floor. It looked as though the floor of the apartment had given way and she could only pray that the damage wouldn't extend to the living room as well. She was just about to suggest to Karen that they moved into the bathroom when a light suddenly appeared through the living room window and the next second a metal cage holding three men swung into view.

Molly felt relief pour through her when she immediately recognised Sean amongst them. There was no time to check if he had seen her, however, because one of the other men was gesturing to her to keep away from the window. She hurried over to the sofa and crouched down beside Karen and the baby, shielding them as best she could as their rescuers broke the window. It took a couple of attempts to break through the toughened safety glass but at last they managed to gain entry. Molly rose unsteadily to her feet, unable to hide her relief when Sean came hurrying over to her.

'Are you all right? Please tell me you're not hurt!'

He gripped her shoulders and her racing heart beat all the faster when she saw the fear in his eyes. No one seeing it could doubt that he had been worried about her, deeply worried too. And that thought seemed to unleash all the emotions she had tried so hard to bury. She wanted Sean to worry about her. She wanted him to care about her safety and wellbeing as she cared about his. She wanted him to feel all those things when he looked at her because she loved him.

Molly took a deep breath as she finally faced up to the truth. For the past two years she had tried to fall *out* of love with him but she hadn't succeeded. She loved Sean every bit as much now as she had ever done, even if he could never love her.

'I'm fine. Really I am.' She forced herself to smile although there was an ache gnawing away inside her. Although there was no doubt in her mind that Sean cared about her, it didn't mean he loved her like he loved Claire. The thought that she could only ever be second best in his eyes hurt unbearably but she couldn't dwell on it. There was too much to do at the present time and she needed to focus on that. 'How soon can we get Karen and the baby out of here?'

'Straight away.' His expression was grim as he glanced at the other woman then turned back to her. 'The crew don't think the building is going to remain standing for very much longer so we need to get everyone out of here as quickly as possible.'

Molly nodded, not needing to hear anything more as she hurried over to Karen and helped her to her feet. One of the crew held the baby while another man helped Karen climb into the cradle, not an easy manoeuvre when there was a yawning drop beneath them. Once Karen was safely seated on the floor of the cradle, they carefully passed the baby to her and then helped Molly step on board. Sean followed next, shaking his head when she asked if they were waiting for the last crew member.

'The cradle will only hold three adults so they'll need to come back for him.'

It seemed to take for ever before they reached the ground although Molly knew for a fact that it was mere minutes. Her legs were trembling when she climbed out and she was glad of Sean's support as she walked shakily over to the ambulance. Karen's husband was already there, waiting for them, and he climbed in as well. Once everyone was safely on board, Sean turned to her.

'You're to go with them.' He shook his head when she opened her mouth to protest. 'No arguing, Molly. You need to get checked over at the hospital.'

'But I'm fine, Sean,' she began then stopped abruptly as he silenced her in the most effective way possible—

with a kiss. Her head was whirling as she climbed into the back of the ambulance because, crazy though it sounded, that kiss had felt as though it had come straight from his heart. What did it mean? Was it possible that Sean loved her after all? She hugged the idea to her all the way back to the hospital, afraid to let it go in case it disappeared into the ether.

It was another half an hour before Sean was finally free to return to the hospital. All the casualties had been seen by then and either sent on their way or transferred to A&E. Amazingly, there had been no fatalities, which was a miracle considering the severity of the accident. The fire crew had the blaze under control now and the air accident investigators were on site. The people who lived in the apartments were being housed temporarily in a nearby hotel so at least they had somewhere clean and safe to sleep tonight. Sean turned to Mac as they left the site together.

'Thanks again for your help, Mac. We wouldn't have fared half as well if you hadn't been here.'

'I was glad to be able to help,' Mac told him, shaking his hand. He sighed as he glanced back at the ruined building. 'It makes you appreciate just how lucky you are when a thing like this happens, doesn't it? Bella used to live in one of those apartments. Thank heaven we moved out when she was expecting Grace. I don't know what I would have done if she'd been caught up in this.'

'Very scary,' Sean agreed soberly, inwardly shuddering at the thought. He understood only too well how it felt to know that the woman he loved was in danger and not be able to do anything about it.

'Too right!' Mac clapped him on the shoulder then headed over to his car. 'Oh, Merry Christmas! I'd forgotten it was Christmas Day in all the chaos.'

'And a Merry Christmas to you too,' Sean replied, smiling as he climbed into the car that was waiting to ferry him and the rest of the team back to the hospital. It was almost five a.m. by then which meant there was barely an hour left before the day shift arrived for duty. He knew that he would be expected to file a report about what had happened during the night but it would have to wait. There was something far more pressing he needed to do at this moment.

Molly was in the staffroom when he tracked her down. She was sitting slumped in a chair with her eyes closed and looked infinitely weary. She had obviously showered since she'd got back because her beautiful red-gold hair was still damp, the riotous curls tumbling around her face and giving her the appearance of one of Botticelli's famous cherubs.

Sean felt a huge wave of love sweep through him as he looked at her. He had come so close to losing her tonight and it had made him see just how much he loved her. He loved her with every fibre of his being, with his heart and his soul, and he wanted to spend the rest of his life showing her how he felt, but was it possible?

Could he leave the past behind and look towards the future—a future which he longed for so very much?

He must have made some sort of a sound because her eyes opened. Sean felt his heart lift when he saw the love that burned in their depths. There wasn't a doubt in his mind that Molly loved him every bit as much as he loved her and it seemed almost too much to know that this kind and beautiful woman was prepared to love him after the way he had behaved towards her in the past.

'Hi!' Her voice was low, gentle, filled with so much love that Sean's heart overflowed with emotion.

'Hi, yourself,' he said, unable to hide how he felt. When she held out her hand, he didn't hesitate; he simply strode across the room and pulled her to her feet. Glancing up, he laughed softly as his eyes alighted on the decidedly wilted bunch of foliage pinned to the ceiling. 'Hmm. That seems propitious. Do you think someone's trying to tell us something?'

'Maybe. Although I doubt if we need anyone's help at this moment, do you?'

Raising herself on tiptoe, she pressed her mouth to his and he sighed deeply. The kiss was filled with so many emotions that he would have needed the best part of a lifetime to sort them all out but he didn't need to do that, did he? Each and every scrap of emotion simply led to one conclusion—that Molly loved him.

He kissed her back, letting his lips tell her exactly how he felt—how much he loved her; how scared he had been of losing her; how he longed for them to be together for ever; and how he feared it might not be possible. And she obviously understood. There was a wealth of sadness in her eyes when she drew back, a pain that cut him to the quick because he didn't want to hurt her, not when he simply wanted to love her.

'Will you come home with me, Sean?' she said quietly and he heard the tremor in her voice and hated himself all the more for making her feel like this. Molly should be rejoicing, filled with happiness at the thought of what the future held in store for them; she definitely shouldn't be experiencing this kind of heartache.

'Are you sure, sweetheart?' His voice caught and he had to force himself to continue but he had to make the situation perfectly clear. 'You must understand that I can't make any promises. I wish I could but...'

'I'm sure.' She pressed her fingers against his mouth, stopping the words because she didn't want to hear them. She gave him a tight little smile. 'I don't expect anything more than you feel able to give me.'

'Oh, Molly!'

Sean drew her to him and kissed her hungrily. That she could be so generous, so giving, was almost more than he could bear.

He let her go when the sound of footsteps alerted them to the fact that the day shift was arriving. He and Molly exchanged pleasantries with several members of staff, brushing aside their eager questions about what had gone on during the night by claiming that they

were too exhausted to talk about it right then. Everyone seemed to accept it so that in a remarkably short
time they were able to leave.

Sean led the way to his car, opening the door for her
while she climbed inside. He slid behind the wheel and
turned to her. 'Happy Christmas, Molly. Let's make this
the best Christmas Day ever, shall we?'

'Yes, let's.'

She smiled back at him, her expression filled with
so much love that he had to stop himself reaching out
and hauling her into his arms. However, this wasn't the
place, he reminded himself as he started the engine.
They needed somewhere a lot more private than the car.

A shudder ran through him at the thought of what
would happen when they got to Molly's house. He and
Molly were going to make love and, although it was
what he wanted more than anything, he knew that afterwards he would have to decide what he intended to
do. It wasn't going to be an easy decision but one thing
was certain: he couldn't leave Molly in a state of limbo.
It wouldn't be fair.

Molly lay in her bed listening to the sound of the
shower running while she remembered all the other
times when this had happened. Sean would be taking
a shower in the bathroom while she lay in her bed and
waited for him…

She blanked out the thought. She didn't want to think
about the past at this moment. Maybe she was burying

her head in the sand but she didn't want any bad memories to taint what was about to happen. When the water stopped and Sean appeared in the bedroom doorway with a towel wrapped around his hips, she smiled. This was what mattered—what happened right now. The past and the future were unimportant.

'Feel better?' she asked as he came over to the bed.

'Much. It's good to get all that muck out of my hair.' He ran his hand over his wet hair, accidentally showering her with water, and she squealed.

'Hey! I've already had a shower this morning. I don't need another one, thank you very much.'

'Sure?' He grinned wickedly as he bent and licked a stray drop of water off her shoulder.

'Uh-huh,' Molly muttered, trying to sound convincing. However, the feel of Sean's tongue licking her skin seemed to have robbed her of even the most basic ability to string several words together.

'Hmm, you don't sound *that* sure to me.'

He deliberately spattered another few drops of water onto her skin, his eyes holding hers as his tongue followed the path they made as they trickled from her shoulder to the edge of the sheet that covered her body. Molly held her breath when he paused then let it out in a whoosh when he pushed aside the sheet, his tongue gliding over her breast until it reached her nipple. Sensations flooded through her when he drew her nipple into his mouth and suckled it.

'Sean!'

His name was an explosion of both sound and feelings as it rushed from her lips and she felt him shudder, felt the hard pressure of his arousal against her hip. When he pushed the sheet completely off her so that his tongue could continue its journey, she didn't protest. Why would she when it was what she wanted, what she needed? She wanted Sean to explore her body and get to know all the dips and hollows again, as she would soon know him.

His tongue had reached her navel now and slowly began to circle it, dipping in and out of the tiny indentation. Molly's hands clenched because each gentle stroke of his tongue against her flesh was merely heightening her desire for an even greater intimacy. When he dragged off his towel and took her hand to wrap it around him, she gloried in the feel of him, so strong and vital beneath her fingers.

'I love you, Molly.' He whispered the words in her ear as he lay down beside her and took her in his arms. 'No matter what happens, I want you to know that this isn't just sex for me.' He kissed her tenderly. 'I love you so very much, my darling.'

'I love you too, Sean,' she told him simply, her heart breaking.

It was unbearably poignant to know that he loved her and still be so unsure about the future. It lent an added urgency to the way they came together. When Sean entered her with one powerful thrust, Molly clung to him, needing to savour every precious second. She had no idea what was going to happen in the future but she refused to allow it to spoil what was happening now. At this moment they had each other. They had everything.

CHAPTER FIFTEEN

THE SOUND OF church bells ringing woke him. Sean lay in bed, feeling strangely at peace with himself. He and Molly had made love not once but twice before they had fallen asleep and he knew that he would store the memory of what had happened in his heart for ever. There had been passion, yes, but as well as that there had been such tenderness that he felt different. Making love with Molly, knowing that there was love in his heart as well as in hers, had been a life-changing experience. Now he knew what he had to do. Knew what he *wanted* to do. And it was a relief to be so sure when he had felt so ambivalent these past weeks. Rolling over, he stroked her cheek, wanting to tell her his decision. Molly had a right to know as this was going to affect her life as much as his.

'Mmm, that feels nice,' she murmured, snuggling against him. 'Has anyone told you that you have magic fingers, Dr Fitzgerald?'

'Nobody who matters,' he replied, replacing his hand with his lips. He trailed a line of butterfly-soft kisses from her ear to her jaw and back again then laughed. 'Come on, sleepy-head, wake up. It's Christmas Day and it's time to rise and shine.'

'Why? Has Santa been?' she retorted, wriggling even closer to him. She chuckled wickedly when she felt his very predictable response to her nearness. 'Maybe that's him knocking at the door right now. I wonder if he has a present for me.'

After a comment like that it was inevitable what would happen. Sean didn't need a second invitation as he gathered her into his arms and kissed her soundly. Their lovemaking was just as fulfilling and as magical this time too and he sighed as he rolled onto his side and looked at her with wonderment.

'How do you make me feel like this, Molly? Have you developed some kind of special powers that I never knew about before?'

'Yes.' She kissed him on the lips, her eyes gentle as she stared at him. 'It's the power of love. It makes everything magical.'

'Oh, sweetheart!' He kissed her this time, feeling desire roaring through him once more. It shouldn't have been possible after what had just happened but they made love again. They were both exhausted when they broke apart. Sean flopped onto his back and groaned.

'My heaven, woman, you're insatiable. You've worn me out!'

'Are you complaining?' she asked cheekily, laughing at him.

'Certainly not!' He grinned back at her. 'Although I may need a breather before you have your wicked way with me yet again.'

'Hmph. Some folk are never happy. It's a good job it's Christmas and the season of goodwill is all I can say.' She tossed back the quilt and got out of bed. 'I shall leave you to recover your strength while I make us some breakfast.'

'I could give it a miss,' Sean offered, grabbing hold of her hand as she went to walk past him. He chuckled because the sight of her naked body seemed to be doing wonders for his flagging libido. 'I may not be *quite* as exhausted as I thought.'

'Too late, stud.' She wriggled out of his grasp and picked up her dressing gown from the back of the chair. 'The only thing you're getting at this precise moment is coffee!'

'Spoilsport,' Sean declared as she swished out of the door with her nose in the air.

He smiled to himself as he sank back against the pillows. It felt marvellous to indulge in this kind of banter and feel so at ease. He had always felt a bit tense when they had been together before, aware that he shouldn't be encouraging any real sense of closeness, but it was different now. He and Molly could relax and enjoy being together without him constantly worrying that he was leading her on. It made it all the more imperative that he carried out that decision he had made.

Sean took a deep breath as he tossed back the quilt,

knowing how hard it was going to be, not only for him but for Claire's parents as well. However, although he hated the thought of upsetting them, the fact was that he couldn't have Molly in his life until he had drawn a line under the past.

Molly put the finishing touches to the breakfast tray and nodded in satisfaction. Freshly squeezed orange juice, eggs Benedict and coffee. There was a platter of fresh fruit as well, although she wasn't sure if it would get eaten or not. As she recalled, breakfast in bed with Sean didn't necessarily involve eating.

Heat rushed through her as she picked up the tray and carried it along the hall. Making love with Sean had been everything she could have wished for. He was both a tender and a passionate lover and she loved how he made her feel. That he enjoyed making love to her wasn't in any doubt but was it enough to tip the scales her way? Maybe he had told her that he loved her but could he leave the past behind? Molly hoped so with every fibre of her being but, as she made her way upstairs, she could feel a sense of dread gathering in the pit of her stomach. A happy-ever-after wasn't guaranteed.

The bed was empty when she reached the bedroom. Molly put the tray on the bedside table, feeling her unease mounting when she heard the shower running again. Why was Sean taking another shower if they were planning to spend the day in bed? When he appeared, fully dressed, she knew that she was right to feel concerned. He was leaving and that didn't bode well, did it?

'Help yourself.' She gestured towards the tray, hoping that he couldn't tell how anxious she felt. It had to be his decision to stay or to go, although it was hard to take such a balanced view.

'It all looks delicious but just coffee for me. Thank you.' He picked up the pot and poured himself a mug of coffee although he made no attempt to drink it.

'Not hungry?' she said lightly, spooning some fruit into a bowl purely for something to do as she doubted if she would be able to eat it when her stomach was churning with nerves.

'Not really.' He took a deep breath and Molly's heart seemed to scrunch up inside her as she waited to hear what he had to say, although she already suspected that it wasn't going to be good news.

'I can't stay, Molly. I'm sorry but there's something I need to do.'

'I see,' she said flatly, leaving it up to him to tell her what was so important that it couldn't wait.

'Yes.' He put his cup back on the tray and reached for her hands. 'I need to speak to Claire's parents, and to my parents, as well, come to that. It's time I told them what really happened the night Claire died.' He squeezed her fingers. 'Then I can put it all behind me.'

'If that's what you want, Sean,' she said, her heart racing with a mixture of fear and excitement. Maybe she was presuming too much but the only reason she could think of why Sean would do such a thing was because of her. Because of them.

'It is.' He bent and kissed her gently on the lips. 'It's what I want more than anything, although I am not looking forward to telling everyone the truth. I know how upset they're going to be.'

The sadness in his eyes was so painful to see. Molly wrapped her arms around him and hugged him tight. 'Are you sure you want to do it today?' she asked quietly. 'I mean, it's Christmas Day and it might make it all the harder for them.'

'Do you think so?' He shook his head. 'I certainly don't want to make it any worse than it has to be for Claire's parents, so do you think I should leave it until tomorrow to go and see them?'

'It's up to you, of course, but it might be easier.' Molly bit her lip, wondering if she was wrong to interfere. It was Sean's decision, after all, but she couldn't bear to think of him piling stress onto stress unnecessarily.

'I think you're right. Christmas Day will be tough enough for them without me showing up and telling them this.' He made a deliberate attempt to lighten the mood, smiling as he glanced at the breakfast tray. 'In which case, I can sample the delights on offer.'

'Food delights, do you mean? Or some other kind?' Molly said, determined to play her part. Maybe it was only putting off the moment until he left her but it would be so good to have this day together, something to remember if things didn't work out as she hoped and prayed they would. She put that dispiriting thought out of her mind as Sean reached for her.

'Both. Although maybe we should start with the *other* delights and carry on from there.'

His mouth was hungry as he kissed her—hungry for her, not for the food that was on offer. Molly kissed him back, showing him through actions rather than words how she felt, how much she loved and needed him. They made love all over again and there was such intensity to their lovemaking that they both cried. Molly kissed away his tears and then he kissed away hers too before they settled down to eat their breakfast. The eggs Benedict were cold and the coffee lukewarm but it didn't matter; it still tasted like manna from heaven because they ate it together, sitting side by side on her bed. Molly prayed with all her heart that there would be other occasions like this in the future but she knew nothing was guaranteed. Until Sean had spoken to everyone then she couldn't be certain that they even had a future.

It was the one black spot in an otherwise wonderful day. After breakfast they went for a long walk down by the river, holding hands and simply enjoying being together. There were quite a lot of people about—parents helping their offspring to ride their brand new bikes, other couples walking hand in hand like they were doing.

Everyone was making the most of Christmas Day, it seemed, and it felt good to be a part of it.

When they got back to her house, Molly started to prepare lunch and Sean helped her, although his idea of helping tended to hold up proceedings. Molly chuckled as she wriggled out of his arms after about the tenth time he had kissed her.

'If you hope to eat today then you have to show some restraint. Not that I'm complaining, mind you. But it's rather difficult to peel sprouts when you're kissing me like that—it's very distracting!'

'Sorry, Chef!' Sean held up his hands in apology. 'I shall behave myself from now on. Promise.'

'Good,' Molly said firmly, although he could tell from the smile that twitched the corners of her gorgeous mouth that she had been enjoying his attentions every bit as much as he had enjoyed lavishing them on her. The thought made him groan and he saw her look at him in surprise.

'What do you want me to do?' he said hurriedly before he managed to break his promise to behave himself. 'I'm a dab hand at peeling sprouts, if you'd like me to do them.'

'All right. If your hands are otherwise occupied then maybe we can eat Christmas dinner actually on Christmas Day.' She handed him the bag of sprouts along with a knife. 'Don't forget to put a cross on the bottom of each one, will you? It helps them cook faster.'

'Yes, Chef!'

Sean saluted smartly, laughing when she rolled her eyes in response. He set to with a will, nevertheless, amazed that something as boring as sprout peeling should be so enjoyable. But there again, why should he be surprised? he thought. Everything he did with Molly took on a whole different light and became much more fun. The thought simply strengthened his determination to sort out his life. No matter how difficult it turned out to be, he had to do it. For him and for Molly.

Especially for Molly.

It was the most wonderful Christmas Day Molly could remember since she was a child. Although they had done nothing more taxing than playing board games after they had finally eaten their dinner, it had been perfect. They had both been on night duty so they had driven into work together in Sean's car. Thankfully, it had been fairly quiet for once so both she and Sean had been able to file their reports about what had happened the previous night. She had even had time to pop up to the Maternity unit to visit Karen and baby Nicholas. Karen's husband was there as well and Molly brushed aside the couple's thanks for what she had done. As she told them truthfully, she had been only too pleased to help.

By the time she finished work, Molly was feeling far more confident about the future. Once again Sean stayed over at her house and they made love again. Although it didn't seem possible, each time they did so, it felt even more wonderful than the time before. She fell asleep, snuggled up against him, feeling happy and sated, and she was still smiling when she woke up in the early afternoon. Being here with Sean was the most perfect experience ever.

Rolling over, Molly went to tell him how she felt but the bed was empty and the sheet on his side was cold when she ran her hand across it. A frisson of alarm scudded through her as she hurriedly got up and dragged on her dressing gown. Surely Sean hadn't left without saying goodbye? Maybe it was silly but she wanted to hold him, kiss him, send him off to do what he had to do knowing how much she loved him.

She ran down the stairs and came to an abrupt halt when she found him in the kitchen, hunched over a cooling mug of coffee. He looked up when he heard her footsteps and smiled but she could see how tense he looked.

'Hi! I hope I didn't wake you up. I tried not to make too much noise.'

'No. It's time I got up,' she said quietly, pulling out a chair. She took a quick breath but the words had to be said. 'Are you going over to see Claire's parents?'

'Yes. I've already phoned my parents and told them I'm coming.' He shrugged. 'It shouldn't take that long. They live just outside Leeds so it's a pretty straightforward drive along the motorway.'

'It shouldn't be that busy today either,' Molly murmured. 'With it being Boxing Day, there won't be as much traffic on the roads.'

'Probably not.' He pushed back his chair and stood up. 'I suppose I'd better get going. I'm in work tonight so I shall need to get back in time for my shift.'

'Of course.'

Molly bit her lip. She wanted to beg him not to go and stay with her but she knew that it would be wrong to do that. Sean had to deal with this in his own way and she mustn't try and stop him because she was afraid of the outcome. When he came around the table and pulled her into his arms, Molly hugged him tightly against her, willing him to feel how much she needed him even though she knew it wouldn't be fair to tell him so at this moment. She mustn't try to influence him in any way.

He didn't say a word as he let her go. Molly sank down onto a chair as he walked along the hall and let himself out of the house, fighting against the urge to run after him. She had to trust him to see this through to the end, no matter how hard it proved to be. Screwing up her eyes, she made a wish that everything would turn out the way she hoped it would. It was Christmas, after all—only good things should happen at this time of the year. But, no matter how hard she tried to cling to that thought, she couldn't stave off the feeling of dread that swept through her. If Sean didn't find the closure he needed then this might be the end for them.

There was no sign of Sean when Molly went into work that night. She had spent the remainder of the afternoon hoping he would phone her but there had been no word from him. She could only assume that he had done what he had intended to do, but it was impossible not to fear the worst. When he appeared some ten minutes after his shift should have started, he looked drawn and grey.

Molly was in the process of taking a case history from an elderly woman who had fainted while having tea with her family. Both her daughters were there and, as they each wanted to have their say about what had happened to their mother, Molly had no choice other than to sit there and listen to them. Nevertheless, she was painfully aware that Sean avoided looking her way as he led his first patient to Cubicles.

She finally sorted out the family and left them in a cubicle while she went to find Steph. It sounded like a severe case of indigestion to her but it wasn't her call and she would leave it to Steph to make the final decision.

Sean was sitting at the computer, updating his patient's notes, and he barely glanced at her. Molly bit her lip but she couldn't face the thought of having to wait any longer to hear what had happened.

'How did you get on?' she said quietly. 'Did you speak to Claire's parents?'

'Yes.' His tone was clipped, not an encouraging sign at all.

'So what happened?' she began then stopped when Jason came over to ask if she would help him with a patient who was refusing to have a booster Tetanus shot.

Molly could hardly refuse, so once she had spoken to Steph she went and sorted out the problem, by which time Sean had disappeared into Resus to deal with a man who had suffered a heart attack. By the time he had finished, she was busily stitching up a woman who had had an accident with a carving knife and cut her hand. And so it went on. Each time Sean was free, she was busy. There was no chance to talk to him, not that he gave any sign that he wanted to talk to her. In fact, it appeared that talking to her was the last thing on his mind and she could only draw her own conclusions from it. Sean had changed his mind and the sooner she accepted that it was over between them, the better.

Sean knew that Molly was desperate to talk to him but he needed time to get everything straight in his head. What he had learned that day had rocked his world. It was only when he saw how drawn Molly looked as she signed out that he realised he had to speak to her. The last thing he wanted was Molly thinking that he had changed his mind about them.

'Can we talk?' he said softly, going over to her.

'If you're sure you want to.' Her eyes met his and he inwardly winced when he saw the hurt they held.

'I am.'

He slid his hand under her elbow, ignoring the curious looks they were attracting from the rest of the staff. Let them think what they liked—it didn't matter. The only thing that mattered was Molly and making sure that she knew how much he loved her. Maybe his world had been rocked but nothing could change that.

The thought helped to relieve some of the shock he had felt ever since he had spoken to both his and Claire's parents. He led her to the car and helped her inside then bent and looked into her eyes. 'I just want to say that what happened today doesn't change a thing. I love you, Molly. And I want to be with you for ever.'

'But?' She gave a hoarse little laugh. 'There has to be a "but" tagged onto the end of that statement.'

'There isn't.' He leant into the car and kissed the tip of her nose. 'I love you and there are no "buts" attached to how I feel either.'

'Then why have you been avoiding me all night long? And don't say that you haven't because we both know it's true. You have done your best not to have to speak to me, Sean, haven't you?'

'Yes, I have,' he admitted. 'And I'm sorry.' He closed the door and walked round to the driver's side, although he didn't immediately start the engine. 'However, I was told something today that I never expected to hear. I needed to get it straight in my own head before I spoke to you.'

'Why? What did they tell you?'

'That Claire had been having an affair with someone she worked with and that the baby might not have been mine after all.'

'What?' Molly stared at him in shock, and he grimaced.

'I know. I was stunned too. I still am. I had no idea that Claire was seeing someone else. Crazy, isn't it?'

He started the engine and drove out of the car park, feeling echoes of the shock he had had that afternoon spreading through him once more. Surely he should have suspected that something had been going on, he thought as he headed along the bypass. Especially when he and Claire had kept arguing all the time. He sighed because it was easy to paint a very different picture of events with the benefit of hindsight. However, the truth was that he had never imagined for a second that Claire had been seeing someone else. He had been far too bound up in making a success of his career to focus on his relationship. He glanced at Molly and felt his heart well up with love. It was a mistake he would never make again.

By tacit consent, they didn't discuss the subject any more until they were back in Molly's house. Molly had needed a bit of time herself to absorb what Sean had told her. She led the way into the sitting room and sank down onto the sofa, wondering what to say to him. It must have been a terrible experience to discover that the woman he had loved so much had been unfaithful to him. Her heart ached at the thought.

'I'm so sorry, Sean,' she said gently as he dropped down into a chair. 'It must have been such a shock for you to hear that. What I don't understand is why your parents, or Claire's, didn't tell you the truth before now. I take it that they knew, so why did they keep it a secret for all these years?'

'Basically because they didn't want to hurt me any more. Both my and Claire's parents decided that it would be better if they didn't tell me immediately after Claire died. And, of course, the longer it went on, the harder it became to tell me the truth.' He shook his head. 'In a weird sort of a way, I can understand their logic but to have let it go on for so long...'

He stopped as though words had failed him, which they probably had. Molly touched his hand, wanting him to know that she was here for him. It was heart-rending to imagine what he must be going through. 'So how do you feel now that you know?' she said softly.

'I'm not sure, to be honest. Shocked, I suppose. Amazed that I never even suspected what was going on. And sad too, because Claire didn't feel able to tell me herself.'

'It must have been awful for you, Sean. I'm so sorry.'

'It wasn't pleasant and if I'd learned the truth even a couple of years ago then I would have been devastated. However, although I do feel shocked because it's completely altered my view of the past, I can see now that if Claire and I had got married then it would never have worked.'

'Really?' Molly exclaimed in surprise.

'Yes.' He captured her hand and raised it to his lips, dropping a gentle kiss on her knuckles. 'I loved Claire very much but I was never *in love* with her. We had grown up together and we were fond of one another, but love? No. It wasn't that. Not as I now understand it.

Maybe she'd realised that too and that is why she had an affair. She sensed that what we had together wasn't the real thing.'

'Are you sure?' Molly had to swallow the knot in her throat. 'You've had a shock, Sean—you've already admitted that. So how can you be sure that your judgement hasn't been affected by it?'

'It's quite simple.' He smiled at her, his face filled with so much love that her heart started to race. 'I know how I feel about you, my darling, and it's very different from how I felt about Claire. I'm in love with you, mind, body and soul, and it is a world removed from anything I have ever felt before.' He stood up and drew her to her feet, enfolding her in his arms and holding her so close that she could feel his heart beating in time with hers.

'It's such a relief that everything is finally out in the open and I don't have this guilty secret burning a hole inside me any more. It means I can now move on, or I can do if you will agree to move on with me, Molly. Will you? Will you take a chance on me, let me love you and care for you for ever and ever?'

'For only as long as that?' she said teasingly.

'How about from here to eternity?' he suggested and then grimaced. 'Sorry! That's the most hackneyed line I could have come up with!'

'Don't you believe it.' She nestled against him, her heart overflowing with happiness. 'Funnily enough, it sounds absolutely perfect to me.'

Lifting her face, she kissed him, wanting to put the

seal on their happiness. Maybe she had stopped believing in happy endings but she had been wrong to do so. She had her very own happy ending right here, although not just an ending but a beginning as well. The beginning of a wonderful new life, loving and living with Sean.

'I love you,' she whispered.

'And I love you too. So very, very much.'

Christmas Eve, one year later...

'Come on, sweetheart, you're nearly there! Just one more push and you'll do it.'

'You want to try pushing,' Molly muttered, screwing up her face as another contraction began. She clung tight hold of Sean's hand as she worked through it, her heart lifting when a second later she heard the tiny cry of a newborn baby. 'What is it—a boy or a girl?' she demanded, lifting herself up on her elbows.

'A boy— a beautiful, perfect little boy,' Sean told her, his deep voice choked with tears. Bending, he kissed her cheek. 'Thank you so much, my love. I didn't think I could be any happier since we got married but I was wrong. Having you and now our son is like having all my dreams come true.'

'Mine too,' she told him, smiling into his eyes.

They had married in the spring, shortly after Molly had discovered that she was pregnant. Sean was surprisingly old-fashioned about such things and had wanted their baby to be born into a traditional family setting.

Everyone had been delighted, Sean's parents and hers—even Claire's parents had sent them a card on their wedding day. It felt as though everyone had moved on and now, with a new baby to celebrate, the future looked rosier than ever.

'So what are we going to call him?' Sean handed the squalling infant to her, perching on the edge of the bed so he could examine his new son's tiny fingers and toes. 'We've changed our minds so many times that I can't remember what we finally decided on.'

Molly laughed. 'It was Sam for a boy, but would you mind if we changed it?'

'Again?' Sean rolled his eyes. 'What to this time?'

'Joseph. It just seems fitting for the time of year, don't you think?'

'Mary and Joseph and the Nativity, you mean?' He nodded. 'Yes, I like it. Joseph Fitzgerald. It has a definite ring to it.'

He picked up the baby's hand and solemnly shook it. 'Welcome to the family, young Joseph. I know that you are going to be very happy because you have the best mum in the whole wide world.'

'And the best dad too,' Molly added, dropping a kiss on the baby's downy head.

* * * * *

MILLS & BOON®
Hardback – December 2015

ROMANCE

The Price of His Redemption	Carol Marinelli
Back in the Brazilian's Bed	Susan Stephens
The Innocent's Sinful Craving	Sara Craven
Brunetti's Secret Son	Maya Blake
Talos Claims His Virgin	Michelle Smart
Destined for the Desert King	Kate Walker
Ravensdale's Defiant Captive	Melanie Milburne
Caught in His Gilded World	Lucy Ellis
The Best Man & The Wedding Planner	Teresa Carpenter
Proposal at the Winter Ball	Jessica Gilmore
Bodyguard...to Bridegroom?	Nikki Logan
Christmas Kisses with Her Boss	Nina Milne
Playboy Doc's Mistletoe Kiss	Tina Beckett
Her Doctor's Christmas Proposal	Louisa George
From Christmas to Forever?	Marion Lennox
A Mummy to Make Christmas	Susanne Hampton
Miracle Under the Mistletoe	Jennifer Taylor
His Christmas Bride-to-Be	Abigail Gordon
Lone Star Holiday Proposal	Yvonne Lindsay
A Baby for the Boss	Maureen Child

MILLS & BOON®
Large Print – December 2015

ROMANCE

The Greek Demands His Heir	Lynne Graham
The Sinner's Marriage Redemption	Annie West
His Sicilian Cinderella	Carol Marinelli
Captivated by the Greek	Julia James
The Perfect Cazorla Wife	Michelle Smart
Claimed for His Duty	Tara Pammi
The Marakaios Baby	Kate Hewitt
Return of the Italian Tycoon	Jennifer Faye
His Unforgettable Fiancée	Teresa Carpenter
Hired by the Brooding Billionaire	Kandy Shepherd
A Will, a Wish...a Proposal	Jessica Gilmore

HISTORICAL

Griffin Stone: Duke of Decadence	Carole Mortimer
Rake Most Likely to Thrill	Bronwyn Scott
Under a Desert Moon	Laura Martin
The Bootlegger's Daughter	Lauri Robinson
The Captain's Frozen Dream	Georgie Lee

MEDICAL

Midwife...to Mum!	Sue MacKay
His Best Friend's Baby	Susan Carlisle
Italian Surgeon to the Stars	Melanie Milburne
Her Greek Doctor's Proposal	Robin Gianna
New York Doc to Blushing Bride	Janice Lynn
Still Married to Her Ex!	Lucy Clark

MILLS & BOON®
Hardback – January 2016

ROMANCE

The Queen's New Year Secret	Maisey Yates
Wearing the De Angelis Ring	Cathy Williams
The Cost of the Forbidden	Carol Marinelli
Mistress of His Revenge	Chantelle Shaw
Theseus Discovers His Heir	Michelle Smart
The Marriage He Must Keep	Dani Collins
Awakening the Ravensdale Heiress	Melanie Milburne
New Year at the Boss's Bidding	Rachael Thomas
His Princess of Convenience	Rebecca Winters
Holiday with the Millionaire	Scarlet Wilson
The Husband She'd Never Met	Barbara Hannay
Unlocking Her Boss's Heart	Christy McKellen
A Daddy for Baby Zoe?	Fiona Lowe
A Love Against All Odds	Emily Forbes
Her Playboy's Proposal	Kate Hardy
One Night...with Her Boss	Annie O'Neil
A Mother for His Adopted Son	Lynne Marshall
A Kiss to Change Her Life	Karin Baine
Twin Heirs to His Throne	Olivia Gates
A Baby for the Boss	Maureen Child

MILLS & BOON®
Large Print – January 2016

ROMANCE

HISTORICAL

MEDICAL